The world is their

area of influence.

The goal is more money

for their pockets.

They always win.

They don't expect any

opposition...until

a bunch of teens

show up.

Also by Walter Dean Myers

WALTER DEAN MYERS

ON A CLEAR DAY

EMBER

Text copyright © 2014 by the Estate of Walter M. Myers
Cover art copyright © 2014 by Ian Keltie

Visit us on the Web! randomhouseteens.com

Educators and librarians, for a variety of teaching tools, visit us at
RHTeachersLibrarians.com

The Library of Congress has cataloged the hardcover edition of this work as follows:
Myers, Walter Dean.
On a clear day / Walter Dean Myers.—First edition.
pages cm.
Summary: In 2035, Dahlia Grillo, a sixteen-year-old math whiz, joins with six other American teens traveling to England to meet with groups from around the world in hopes of stopping C8, the companies that control nearly everything for their own benefit.
ISBN 978-0-385-38753-8 (hardcover) — ISBN 978-0-385-38754-5 (library binding) — ISBN 978-0-385-38755-2 (ebook) [1. Social action—Fiction. 2. Interpersonal relations—Fiction. 3. England—Fiction. 4. Science fiction.] I. Title.
PZ7.M992On 2014
[Fic]—dc23
2013046708

ISBN 978-0-385-38756-9 (pbk.)

Printed in the United States of America

10 9 8 7 6 5 4 3 2 1

First Ember Edition 2015

ON A CLEAR DAY

1

"She just stopped singing." Ernesto, María's husband, was a thin, yellowish man with a wisp of a mustache. He wiped at his face as we sat in the back of his old Ford. "That's what she liked to do best," he went on, talking to himself as much as to the rest of us, "singing and sometimes dancing even when there wasn't any music."

María Esteban was only thirty-eight when she died. When she stopped singing. She was my cousin and had taken care of me after my mother died. Once we had been close. She had let me do her hair sometimes and laughed when I messed it up. Then we had grown apart, or maybe had both begun to withdraw into ourselves, the way poor people seemed to do more and more. I remembered her singing as we walked down Fox Street to our little house. I didn't remember her stopping her songs.

The pickup truck and the three cars that made up the small funeral procession moved slowly down Mosholu Parkway toward Van Cortlandt Park.

"She always used to sing. I should have known," Ernesto said, more to himself than to anyone else. "I should have known."

It was getting harder to tell when people were going to die. There weren't many warning signs. Sometimes a slight cough into a handkerchief, perhaps a distant look in the eyes, but mostly it was just a turning inward. They had simply given up on life. They had forgotten their songs. When I saw someone giving up, I wondered if, one day, I would give up too.

The casket was in the back of the pickup truck. It looked like metal, but I knew it was corrugated cardboard. Around it were a few sad flowers, pictures cut out from religious calendars and framed, and candles. Yes, and signs printed out in Magic Marker that read "Rest in Peace," or "We Love You, María."

Old people said that Van Cortlandt Park had been a happy place once. There had been picnics and children playing and families everywhere. I couldn't imagine it. Now it was just a dreary place, a place where we went to dispose of the dead.

Our little convoy stopped and two men—I thought they were probably from St. Athanasius, María's church—took the casket from the truck and placed it on the concrete platform in front of the old band shell. Even before the priest got there, the two men had begun to pour water into the openings at the foot and the head of the casket. Biocremation took only twenty minutes if everything went right. Oxygen-infused potassium hydroxide lined the casket, the water was poured in, and in seconds, the body would begin to decompose. We wanted to honor María Esteban, but no one wanted to be away from our neighborhood for too long. It wasn't safe.

I had read historical accounts of bodies cremated by burning. It would have been better, I thought. We could have seen the flames rising to the heavens. We could have pretended the body was going to someplace called Heaven.

A priest was praying in Spanish for María's soul while another man—short, square, baggy pants—held a shotgun as he nervously looked around for any *favelos*, roaming gangs who might be in the area.

Then the priest's prayer was over, and the dead woman's neighbors were getting into their cars. The city would send their crews to clean up the final remains of my cousin. I watched as tiny birds made black silhouettes against the steel-gray sky.

"Dahlia, it's time to go." Alfredo, the owner of the bodega on my corner, spoke softly.

"I'm not going back," I said impulsively.

"You don't have any other place to go," Alfredo answered. He smelled of garlic and tobacco. He put his hand on my shoulder, and I turned away. "Try not to stay out too late. In any case, we'll wait up for you."

As the cars rolled away, I saw the mourners' faces against the glass windows. I knew they would understand how I felt. They would think about me and María as they drove the six miles back to our own little section of *el barrio*. And I knew they would save my place.

María had been a cousin and a friend. She knew how to touch me, and when to put her arm around my waist and smile at me even when her own life was not going well. More than that. More than that, she knew how not to dig too deep for the truth when the truth wasn't worth a damn, which was most of the time.

Years ago I read Fanon's book *The Wretched of the Earth*. Good shit, mostly. We, me, María, everybody in the Bronx, we were the wretched of the earth, wandering through our lives like sheep in a storm, struggling to make sense of what was not sensible. I was feeling sorry for myself.

Good. I liked feeling sorry for myself.

I began to walk without any thought to where I was going. Through my tears, the late-summer light broke up into shards of color that made everything seem unreal. It was almost beautiful. Almost as if that was the way to look at life in 2035.

I felt sorry for María, and for myself. For a wild moment I imagined I was in my own corrugated casket, engulfed in flames. Then I stopped and got mad at myself for going there. I got mad at María, too. She needed to be stronger. She knew that.

I was cold and pulled my sweater tighter across my chest. Looking around, I began to feel fear. Back in my own community, I was frustrated and lonely. Away from those crumbling tenements, I was open to attack. What would I do if I encountered a group of *favelos* wandering through the park? Or Sturmers?

The Sturmers, as they called themselves, were mercenaries who sold out to the highest bidder. They dressed and acted like Nazi storm troopers and even used a variant of *"Stürmer,"* like the German term, for some of their troops. They managed to hate everything and everybody, but they were cruel enough to negotiate through the screwed-up world that the C-8 companies had created.

I turned and headed out of the park, the way the cars from the funeral had gone. I walked quickly. I was cold. It began to rain.

It was dark when I reached Fox Street. The streets were shiny from the rain, and the neon lights reflecting off the black pavement were almost festive. The guards at the gate waved me through. I knew I didn't have anything at home to eat except wild rice, but all I needed was tea. I walked up the two flights in semidarkness, opened my door, went in quickly, and locked the door behind me.

Hello, yellow walls. Hello, green curtains flapping against the window. Hello, roaches.

I touched my computer screen, navigated to a puzzle, memorized it quickly, and then put the water on for tea. Chai and ginger. It would chase away the cold.

And then I was crying again, and being mad at myself for crying, and glad for the relief it brought me. There was nothing else to do and be sane. I lay across the narrow bed and closed my eyes, waiting for the sound of the kettle to comfort me.

I was so friggin' down. My narrow bed seemed even smaller than usual, and there was no position that felt comfortable. The streets outside were quiet except for an occasional truck that rumbled past. I started counting again. I hated the counting, but I did it almost every night. One bed, one dresser, one built-in closet, one chair, one lamp, a table where my computer sat, winking at me, one basin, one sink, one small microwave oven. In the tiny bathroom there was another sink, a john, a medicine cabinet where I kept my toothbrush, baking soda, soap, and flash drives.

Think of something else. I closed my eyes and imagined that I was in the back of the pickup truck. It was slowing, and soon they were lifting me onto the concrete slab where I would be disintegrated. I was glad to have it over with, to move to some other plane. I was glad, but in the stillness of my room, I was crying.

One bed, one dresser, one built-in closet, one chair, one lamp, a table where my computer sat, one basin, one sink, one small microwave oven. In the tiny bathroom there was another sink, a john, a medicine cabinet where I kept my toothbrush, baking soda, soap, and flash . . .

The window was open slightly, and the coolness of the night air felt delicious as it made the tiny hairs on my ankles stand up. Delicious because it was a feeling. It told me that I was still alive. Barely.

My name is Dahlia Grillo. I am sixteen. There was a time when I looked forward to being seventeen. My mother had me at seventeen, and I thought I would go past that age and become something great, even though I didn't know what something great could be. Perhaps a math teacher. I liked to imagine myself teaching little kids geometry and watching them discover things about triangles and the relationships between angles. When I was thirteen, and fourteen, and just getting comfortable with my period, I knew I had to be serious about life. But being serious about your life meant getting real with your dreams. Some of my friends wanted to be singers, or actresses, and I didn't say much about that but I knew it wasn't going anywhere.

All that changed in a friggin' heartbeat. It was like there was a plan to have a surprise party for everybody—how weird does that sound?—and then, at the last minute, they decided to kick the crap out of everybody instead.

We had all known about the Central Eight companies. C-8 controlled everything, and some people were worried about just how much influence they had, but it was the way they screwed with your head that got to me. Like when one of the companies claimed that they could end world hunger within ten years and announced a quadrillion-dollar investment. The Internet was all over that, saying that it would bring an end to war and an end to dictators and an end to everything bad except dandruff. The company brought out a whole new range of seeds that could grow anywhere and bugs couldn't mess with. But then they got a patent on the seeds, and before anyone knew it, they controlled all the food production in the world. And people were starving everywhere.

It was bad, but it wasn't so bad if it didn't reach you personally.

"The sun is always warm if your belly is full!" my mother used to say. Poor mama. After my father died, she worked so hard to find a better life. When things began to come apart, when people started noticing which category they fell into, she worked even harder to keep us out of the lowest rank. That's how we got to Fox Street in the Bronx.

The lowest rank was the *favelos*, poor people who lived by either stealing or begging. Nobody knew how many of them there were. Some people said that in America, it was half the population.

The next step up was the Gaters, people who lived in gated communities. At first they just built communities with their own shopping malls and restaurants away from the inner cities, places you needed a car to get to. Then they started issuing special credit cards if you wanted to buy anything in their communities. And finally they put up gates and armed guards. My neighborhood, *mi barrio loco*, had gates even though no one had much money and the dried-up old men guarding them were mostly useless. Still, they wanted to keep the *favelos* out because they'd steal whatever little we had.

Mama worked two jobs to buy an apartment just for the two of us. I knew she was working herself to death. When she died, my family bought our apartment and gave me the little place I have now rent-free.

So there are the *favelos*, then the Gaters, then those invisible people who seem to have everything. The *New Yorker* magazine always has articles about how unfair it is for some tiny percentage of the population to own everything. But just knowing something doesn't help you to do anything about it when you're too busy trying to cover your own butt. You saw what was going on, and then after a while—maybe your mind closed down or something, I don't know—you stopped seeing it.

Nobody saw the whole school thing coming. Well, maybe some people saw it, but I sure didn't.

It started when the government announced that it was going to increase the educational opportunities for everybody and make the whole system fairer. Then we heard that everyone was going to get the new supertablets and individual instruction in any field you wanted. Free. That was like really great. All these trucks started pulling up and unloading boxes of electronic stuff and passing it out like it was free candy or something.

What came to my mind was that there were so many around, the *favelos* wouldn't steal them. The tablets were good. They had all the connections you needed, but the apps were just so-so. If you knew what you were doing, you could fix the apps, and I did. What I couldn't fix, what blindsided me, was when they closed the schools. I was almost fifteen.

What did you need schools for if the curriculum apps were available? You could go over and over the material until you got it in your head, and the FAQ sections were intuitive and generally on the money. I took advanced math courses and dug them, but I missed hanging out in school. The word on the street was that the higher-level Gaters were hiring private tutors. The rest of us were on our own. It was nothing new, once you thought about it. It just was smack up in our faces for the first time.

I don't know what it was about hanging out with other kids in school that was so good. I learned as much about the subjects I liked from the apps as I would have sitting in a classroom. But when school actually shut down I felt terrible. Something deep inside of me was going crazy, as if I was having trouble breathing. A friend said it was just because we were getting older, that letting go of being a kid was hard. I don't know, maybe she was right.

I used to look forward to being seventeen. Now it doesn't seem like such a big deal. If seventeen happens, it happens.

2

Every day for the next week I watched the minutes pass, and then the hours. The light outside my window changed the color of the ancient blinds from pale yellow to gray to charcoal brown as the sun slanted from across Rainey Park. María's death pushed in on me, squeezed me against the walls, and I realized how quiet I had become. *She just stopped singing,* Ernesto said. That was what America had become. In the old films, families chatted around the dinner table, making smart-ass remarks over canned laughter and twisting their faces to show what you were supposed to think. I loved the old films because the people in them were so uncomplicated. It was as if they had nothing really to care about.

I thought that I had nothing really to care about.

Footsteps on the stairs. *Clunk, tap. Clunk, tap.* It was Ramón, and by the rhythm of his steps, I could tell he was in a hurry. Perhaps his toilet was stopped up again and he wanted to use mine. He would pee all over it and I'd have to scrub it down.

"Girl!" he called in a hoarse voice. "Girl!"

I got up quickly, moved across the floor in the darkness, and turned on the lamp. My bathrobe was hanging on the door, and I threw it around my shoulders. Through the open door I saw his half-moon face close to me. His eyes were dark and shining. There was a fear in his manner.

"What?" I asked.

"Two boys down there," he said. He pointed with a bony finger toward the floor. "They ask for you."

"They said my name?"

"Yes!" He nodded furiously and his eyes grew wide.

I thought of going back to bed, of ignoring whoever it was, but I knew I would never go to sleep. Who were they? Maybe the old man was wrong and they didn't know my name. Maybe they were just asking for a girl.

"What did they say?"

"They said Dahlia Grillo!" The bony finger was pointing up. "You can run to the roof and come down in the back where the cleaner's used to be!"

"What do they look like?"

"One is in a wheelchair, and the *pájaro* is walking!" The

old man wiped at his chin. "Rafael is downstairs. He has a pistol in his jacket."

A wheelchair?

"I'll come down. Tell Rafael not to go away."

"You should run!"

"What do they want?"

"Maybe they're looking for a woman."

"One in a wheelchair and the other is gay? I don't think so."

I put on my jeans and a sweater and followed the old man downstairs. He stopped every few steps and peered down, like a cat. The smell of fried garlic came up to meet us, and I felt better.

From the window on the first floor I saw them. Two white boys. They were in the street next to a small van. It looked like some kind of military vehicle. Wheelchair Boy looked anxious. The other one sat on the bumper and had one leg crossed over the other. He looked freaky. I went downstairs and to the front door. Rafael was standing near the front gate. His hand was in his pocket, and I knew he was holding his gun.

The boys looked at me. I couldn't tell how old they were, but they were young. The one who the old man described as gay seemed confident. Either he had beautiful eyes or he was wearing eyeliner. His hair was streaked with colors.

"Who are you looking for?" I asked.

"Someone who wrote an article on computer projections for the *Math Journal*," Wheelchair Boy said. "Dahlia Grillo. Do you know her?"

"Maybe," I said. "Who are you?"

"My name is Javier."

"Michael," the other one said.

For a moment I thought they were making up the names, but then a flash hit me and I wanted to look up again at the boy who was standing. I thought I knew him.

"Why do you want to see this . . . what did you say her name was?" I was not looking up.

"Dahlia Grillo," Javier said. He was smiling slightly. I didn't like him.

"Why do you want to see her?"

"You live here," the other boy said. "You know what is going on in the world. How screwed up things have become. But there are people who want to change things. Mostly young people."

He looked away, down the street. I checked to see what he was looking at, and there wasn't anything to see. We looked back at each other and he started talking again.

"There's going to be a conference in London of people from around the world who have the idea that we can save the world. I've been invited to the meeting and want to bring some people with me. Very bright people who want to redirect the way the world works. There's a bit of a crisis going on. The Central Eight—you know who I'm talking about?"

"Maybe."

"Maybe? Okay. They've leaked a report, or maybe it was hacked, that they expect a two-percent growth in the economy next year. They've been feeding us zero growth for years as some kind of balanced utopia, and now they're going to start heating things up again. That's got to be either impossible to pull off or very painful for somebody else. Or it could mean that C-8 is going to expand."

He stopped and looked at me.

"So?"

"So the Eton Group—that's what the Brits call themselves—is organizing the conference to see what can be done," Michael said. "I would like to take an American team with me. Seven or eight good people who care about doing something positive. I hoped that Dahlia Grillo would be part of that team."

"From what we've heard, she has mind-blowing math skills." Javier spoke again. "Someone in California saw an article she wrote in the *Math Journal*. She's smart enough, but we're leaving for the UK in two days, so we need her on board quickly."

"If I see her, I'll tell her," I said.

"I've got a handout you can show her," Michael said. "If she's interested, there's a number she can call. We need the best people we can get. I know the Brits are sharp, and I know they can't handle the job by themselves. There are people all over the planet forming small resistance groups. The C-8 companies know about us, but they don't see us as a threat. And I guess we haven't been up to now. But if the two-percent figure is right—I just want to know whose veins they're going to take it from . . ."

His voice trailed off. He looked serious.

"We'll wait for her call," Javier said.

"Who is 'we'?" I asked. "Who are you?"

"I'm somebody who thinks that a group of us can make a difference," Michael said. "I'm getting together other people who at least want to try. Or maybe they see that doing nothing when you see evil means that eventually you become part of that evil."

"Could be," I said.

"You don't trust us." Javier was smiling again. "That's a good sign. Trust isn't worth a lot these days."

"Neither are words," I said, wishing I hadn't.

"Yeah, that's true, but if you happen to see Dahlia"—Michael stood and extended his hand to me—"tell her we really need her."

"You say the English call themselves the Eton Group," I said. "What do you call yourselves?"

"The Resistance." Javier spoke quickly.

"Not very original," I said.

Michael shrugged and held out his hand again. It was soft and cool to the touch.

I looked away from his eyes.

Then they started to leave. The old man and Rafael stood at the door, watching them. I turned and saw Mrs. Rosario looking out the doorway. We watched as the motorized wheelchair went into the back of the van they were driving. It looked like Wheelchair Boy was getting into the driver's seat.

"You want me to run and shoot them?" Rafael asked.

"Not yet," I said, smiling.

Rafael smiled back. He told me not to trust them. "They don't know you are Dahlia," he said. "They come tomorrow and we'll tell them we don't know her or you."

I kissed the old man and shook Rafael's hand. He took the pistol out of his pocket and showed it to me. It was old and rusted around the barrel.

"If you need me . . . ," he said.

"Yes," I answered.

3

I rushed upstairs and to my dresser. Bottom drawer. Photos. A folded program from my mother's funeral. Two notebooks. Then, still in the manila envelope they came in, two copies of the *Math Journal*. My heart was beating faster as I opened the envelope and turned to the page where I had not resisted the urge to put in a bookmark. There, under a picture of me trying to smile, was my name—Dahlia Grillo.

They had seen my picture. They had known who I was.

Footsteps in the hall. For a wild moment I thought it was the boys coming up the stairs, but then I recognized the pattern of the steps. Mrs. Rosario.

"You shouldn't be alone," she said. "Come down and help me cook."

I didn't want to cook, but I wanted to be with Mrs. Rosario. She reminded me of my Dominican heritage more than anyone I knew. She was memory in the way she walked, the way she moved.

She took me by the arm. She smelled of onions and garlic, and my arm felt good against the side of her heavy chest. We went down to her apartment, and it was warm and inviting. My mind was racing, and I could feel the excitement in my legs. The boys had read my article on computer modeling and said they wanted me. If they had pushed me harder, if they had said "Come right now!" I might have done it.

We cooked. I was cutting up the meat. Mrs. Rosario said that it was pork, but the small bones told me that it was goat.

"One time, maybe a thousand years ago, two boys came to visit me." Mrs. Rosario's voice was low, husky. The voice of a woman who had lived. "They wanted me to go camping with them. They were going to climb some mountain—Pico Duarte, I think, I don't know. I had to ask my mama, but I had to ask in a way that made it seem like I didn't want to go. You know what I mean?"

"Did you want to go?"

"No, because I thought they just wanted to do the bang bang with me," Mrs. Rosario said. "I didn't want to do that, but at the same time I wanted to go. My mother grabbed a wooden spoon and chased them from the house.

"They took another girl, a skinny girl named Lisette, and they went off for a whole week!"

I put flour on the goat meat and dropped it into the

heavy skillet. It sizzled nicely as I pushed it around with a fork.

"When I was very little," Mrs. Rosario said, "a woman told me that women in love always cooked with their fingers in the pot. I used to turn the meat with my fingers. You get lots of nice burned fingers that way."

"So what happened to the other girl?" I asked.

"Nothing. She swore it and I believed her, but her reputation was ruined anyway. No woman in our village thought the same of her after that. I think they felt as I did. We were mad at her but a little envious too."

"You were lucky you didn't go," I said.

"That girl was stronger than I was, but her reputation was ruined," Mrs. Rosario said. "All my life I wished I had gone with those boys. I think of it a hundred times a year. Most of the time I imagine being out there in the rain, on Pico Duarte, and being cold and shivering as I huddle between them. Even today I love the taste of rain. It brings back memories of what I just imagined. Isn't that strange? Nothing happened, but you remember what you thought might have happened?"

We took the seared meat out of the pan and put it in a bowl as the cooking garlic filled Mrs. Rosario's kitchen with its magic odors. I scraped the pan and put the little bits into the bowl with the meat.

"Don't be afraid of adding salt," Mrs. Rosario said. "When you're cooking, a time comes when you have to take a chance. With the spices, with life."

My mind was already racing ahead, much too fast for

me, much too close to the edges. Thinking became impossible even as I kept telling myself to think.

I put salt and red pepper on the meat and put it back into the black iron skillet in big handfuls. Mrs. Rosario pushed the meat around with a wooden spoon until each piece had touched the hot iron of the ancient pan again. Then we added the canned tomatoes and oregano. More stirring. We turned the heat down and poured cold chicken broth into the center. It smelled good, and I thought that maybe I would eat it.

She talked as she mashed some of the chickpeas with chili flakes, adding just enough water to make them mushy. Woman stuff. Good.

"Not too much, not too much," she said as she lifted the salt with her fingertips from her palm and sprinkled it on the meat.

I knew the mushy chickpeas would go in first, and then the whole ones later. The fragrant smells were filling me up, comforting me.

"Did you ever speak to the girl?" I asked.

"To Lisette?"

"Yes."

"At first she was upset because people thought of her as a bad girl." Mrs. Rosario leaned against the table. "Then she began to walk with her head up and her back straight and look everyone in the eye. When I spoke to her, she said, 'Who I am is who I am!'"

When we were finished cooking, Mrs. Rosario called in the old man and Rafael. Rafael brought a young girl with him. She was eight, maybe nine. She sat at the far end of the table, at Rafael's elbow, and bent her head slightly forward to see me at the other end.

The old man was talking about the van the boys had come in. He said that it was probably an old army vehicle.

"Maybe bulletproof!" he said with a nod.

"You can always shoot the driver," Rafael said. "Even if the glass is shatterproof, a good bullet goes right through."

The little girl was looking at me, watching me. Big, dark eyes that questioned me from five feet away. Who was I? Would she be like me one day? I was closest to her age. I was the next step in her life.

"They might have got your name from the school records," Rafael said. "They're selling the lists of students to private teachers. They sell everything these days."

Mrs. Rosario was watching me too. She was thinking about the time when she could have gone away with some boys.

And who were these boys? I had glanced at the handout they had given me. It was the same crap that everybody knew about. The Central Eight had become a huge force that ruled the universe. If C-8 had been around at the time of the Incas, virgins would have been sacrificed in the volcanic heat of their power. C-8 postured like they were some kind of modern gods, while the poor, the old, the millions of children scurrying like roaches around the world were supposed to thank them for their very existence. Taking C-8 down wasn't the work for strange boys with a half-assed idea.

There had been other groups that had tried to stand up to the Central Eight. They had protested in mass meetings, had locked arms and tossed flowers at the police, had done all the crap people did, and then had gone away to their own little holes. The boys had said they were going to a conference somewhere. Big deal. What difference did it make? They would be beaten back, knocked down. Maybe killed if they were too convincing. What difference did anything make anymore?

Like my cousin, they would see the futility of it all and stop singing.

But the boys had asked for me. They had known my name, had read my piece in the *Math Journal*. I was breathing faster just thinking about it. What were they going to do? I thought of Mrs. Rosario thinking about the boys who had come for her. What would she have done in my situation? What was she telling me to do?

I remembered Michael. He had fronted a band known as Plato's Cave, or something like that. It was hot for about three years and he had made buckets of money with music the zines had called the Flare sound. They'd start with one melody over a hard driving beat, follow that up with a different melody over a counterbeat, and then bring them closer and closer together until they overlapped. It was edgy and frantic and I liked it a lot. Then, in the middle of a concert in Australia, Michael had walked away from it all. Some people said he had just made enough money, and some said he was working on something new, but his band died after that. I heard he had been accused of supplying money to some kids in Oregon who were protesting something, but that didn't make the papers for more than a day or two. Hardly anything did anymore.

The boy in the wheelchair looked as if he had money. His clothes fit too well; his haircut was too perfect for him to be poor. He had something going on. I didn't know what.

But what if their shtick wasn't real? What if they had their own separate agendas and just wanted to use me? What would I do? Or say?

"I do math," I would say. "I don't fuck."

Rafael was wiping his plate with a roll he had broken in half, sopping up the gravy. The girl was still scoping me out. I looked at her and smiled, but she didn't smile back.

How had the boys expected me to react when I read the literature they gave me? Hadn't they noticed that anger wasn't in anymore? That only the struggle to survive had real meaning?

For a moment I was mad at the boys, but I couldn't stop the feeling of excitement coming over me. I felt like a starving person waiting for a wonderful meal to be cooked. I didn't want to wait. I wanted to start eating.

Mrs. Rosario kept talking. I think she was afraid that when she stopped, I would leave. She needed to talk, and I understood that. She said we might have used too many tomatoes.

"It's just right!" Rafael protested.

"Better than that!" the old man said.

"What do you think, Lydia?" Mrs. Rosario asked the girl.

"It's nice" was her answer. A trace of a smile flickered across her face. She was wearing braces.

There was still some yellow rice left, and a few plantains. It was so good. When everything was finished, when the old man and Rafael and little Lydia had left, I helped Mrs. Rosario clean up and she hugged me tightly.

"You always have to be careful with boys," she warned. "Whatever you do, keep your soul in your mind."

I walked slowly up to my room and looked at the handout again. I started to read it, but there was nothing new in it, so I put it down. Then I took out my article in the *Math Journal* and looked at my picture. Pushing my hair back as I looked in the mirror, I saw that I was the same. Almost pretty.

I cloud-groped the Eton Group on the Internet and got nothing. Eton came up as a place in the UK, and I knew it from crossword puzzles. A school that had been for boys but that was now a big deal for the children of the British elite. A pop-up ad asked if I wanted to go there.

I was completely conflicted. One part of me was cautious, scared. Another part felt that nothing they could do would work. It was all hopeless.

I thought of Mrs. Rosario's story. She was still longing for the adventure she'd never had. I thought of the girl. Lisette. A lovely name. A name Mrs. Rosario still remembered after so many years.

Options. What were my options? Get a job and hope to improve my life. Be good at something and always have food to eat and a safe place to stay. Then how did I call that life? What would I do to pretend I was doing more than stringing along the moments of my existence? Maybe I could get ahead and do better than the people around me. I knew I was smart. What did my math professor say? "Most people take ten to the third power and are glad to reach one thousand. But the smartest people take ten to the power of pi, and they are always ahead, always moving faster than the rest."

It had pleased him to say that, but I hadn't seen anything in it. Life was personal, not a friggin' competition.

Before my mother died, I sat with her in the hospital. She was crying because she had nothing to leave me. She said she could give me a small piece of advice if I wanted it. *If I wanted it?* I wanted anything from her at that sad moment, a touch, a kiss.

"Know what's in your heart," she said. "Not just what's in your head."

In my heart, I knew I was going with the boys.

The rail at the edge of the bed hurt my butt as I sat on it. I knew if María had still been alive, she would have warned me to be careful.

"Make sure you got your big-girl panties on," she would have said. But she wasn't alive. She had given up, had let her song disappear somewhere between the *mercado* and her apartment.

Punching in the number they had given me, 8-5-8-9-8-6-9-0-5-6, I recognized it as a perfect number and wondered if they had paid extra for it. I heard some clicks and tones, and I could tell that the call was going through a series of towers. Maybe so it wouldn't be traced.

"Hello?"

"This is Dahlia," I said weakly.

"This is Javier" came the too-quick reply. "We can send a car for you tomorrow at five in the morning. Is that too early?"

"No."

"Don't bring too much," Javier said. "It's better that way. We can get anything you need later. You take any meds?"

"No."

"Then I'll see you in the morning."

"Fine."

"And I would just tell people you absolutely trust," he said.

"I don't have anything to tell, do I?"

"I guess not." His voice softened. "I'm glad you're aboard."

"You think we're going to make some kind of difference?" I asked.

"Michael says it doesn't matter," Javier said. "It's the attempt that counts."

"Oh, okay."

The phone was lying on the bed. I was telling myself that I didn't care what happened and trying to keep my food down. I looked up Cataldi, the Italian mathematician who had worked with perfect numbers, and found that he lived from 1548 to 1626. He was seventy-eight when he died. I loved the idea of having all that time to do the work you cared about.

I wanted to tell Mrs. Rosario that I was going. And Rafael. All of them. Maybe even find Ernesto and tell him. What difference did it make? We weren't real Gaters, living behind electrified fences with guards ready to shoot people. We were pretenders, poor people banding together in the Bronx behind a fence that didn't mean a thing, guarded by old men who hadn't fired a shot since they'd been through the country's military machine.

Thinking about taking a shower. Or wait until morning? Take one now in case I oversleep in the morning.

In the shower. There was sand on the bottom of the tub. I didn't like the feeling of grit under my bare feet and didn't feel like washing the tub out. Make the shower quick, then out and dry off. I thought about telling Mrs. Rosario that I was going off with the boys and already felt her arms around me. In my mind it was a good feeling.

Packing. Don't take too much. I didn't *have* too much. Three pairs of jeans, all I owned. Six tops, all I owned. Three bras, eight pairs of panties, six pairs of socks, one hat, and my jacket. Everything went into my red backpack. It was most of what I owned.

So now I was lying on my bed and thinking about what Mrs. Rosario was going to say.

"Are you going to be the only girl?"

Shit, I should have asked that! Should I call back? And if they said I'd be the only girl, what would I do? Say that I was afraid?

Maybe I should be afraid.

I was going—fuck it.

Sleep was not going to happen. I stared off into the darkness and tried to remember to breathe from my lower belly. I checked the clock over and over and the hands moved slower and slower. I set the alarm for four-thirty, then switched it to four. I could just leave without saying anything to Mrs. Rosario. Yes, that was what I'd do. She'd see that I was gone and know that everything was cool with me.

The conversations played like recorded messages. Michael was looking at me with his weird eyes, knowing who I was but trying to figure out who I really was beyond the one article he'd read.

"Are you going to be the only girl? Are you going to be the only brown person?"

Javier was white white, almost pale. Michael was white with darkness around his eyes and colors in his hair. When I had asked Javier if he thought we were going to make a difference, he had said—no, he'd mumbled—that Michael didn't think it mattered. Were Michael and Javier going out? I didn't want to be a part of that.

What did I want to be a part of?

I jerked awake. What time was it? In the darkness, the clock just touched my fingers before it clattered across the floor. Up, switch the light on, find the damned clock. Two thirty-six. Stay awake. No, I'll be exhausted before the day even begins.

Back to bed. Sleep for a minute. Check the time. Two fifty-five. Crap.

Thinking about my mother. Always sad, like a flower badly in need of water but never getting it, always drooping, so after a while I felt that was the way she was supposed to look. Wistful eyes that never found mine until that last day, when she knew she was leaving forever.

Know what's in your heart. . . .

There must have been a time when, somewhere deep inside of me, I knew that I didn't want to be my mother. It must have shown up for an instant, must have sprung up between us like a sudden storm, catching us by surprise. Or was it just me? Did she see it in my eyes?

Mama, I don't ever want to be you!

Think of something else. Think of all the online courses I was considering. A thousand Introductions to EveryFriggin'Thing and me trying to map out a Learning Intelligently Pattern. What I came up with was that school without the hustle and bustle of other kids didn't make any sense. I didn't want to be smart; I wanted to learn *with* somebody. But why, when that wasn't really me? When I was best by myself, except for all the times when being by myself got me down. Why did I need other kids around?

"It's like jazz," my teacher had said. "It's good by yourself, but it's a lot better with friends."

Jerk awake. Turn on the light. Check the time. Four-fifteen. A moment of panic. I'm up! I'm dressed. Check the time. Four-eighteen. Oh, okay.

My backpack was ready and by the door. I went to the bathroom and rinsed my mouth with salt water. Then downstairs to Mrs. Rosario. I knocked on the door and in seconds she was asking who it was.

"Dahlia."

She opened the door and saw I was dressed.

"I'm going with the boys this morning," I said.

She hugged me and pulled me into her apartment. "You're going to be all right," she said.

"I know," I said, not knowing. I was crying and she was crying and wiping away my tears with her stubby fingers.

"I have something for you," she said.

She went to the ancient chest and opened the bottom drawer. For a moment she rummaged through it, and then she pulled out a piece of material and held it up to the yellow lamplight.

It was a shawl, long and lacy, and white. I could see through it, but toward the center there were two perfect roses. When she placed it over my shoulders, there was a rose on each side of me.

"You look beautiful," she said. "Think of me when you wear it, Dahlia. Will you think of me?"

"Yes," I said. "Yes."

5

Five o'clock. The car arrived. Clunky. Square. There was armor on the sides. I was nervous as I approached it. The window went down and a young guy turned his round face toward me.

"Good morning, Miss Grillo."

"Good morning." The air was cold and damp. The young guy was out of the car, shorter than I imagined him to be. Asian, perhaps. He took my bag and flung it into the back.

He looked at me and opened the rear door. I could feel my heart beating crazily as I climbed in. Turning, I saw Mrs. Rosario standing in the doorway. Beside her, a thin white arm around her waist, was the girl who had been at dinner. In the morning light, with her gown clinging to her skinny legs, she looked like a pale angel. I waved to her. She didn't move.

"Your seat belt."

I fastened the seat belt, and we took off.

I said, or thought I said, something about it being a cool morning. The driver didn't answer. Maybe I didn't say it. We drove quickly, almost furiously, across the Bronx and then south toward the George Washington Bridge. Every doubt that I had buried came to mind. But I kept telling myself that it didn't matter what happened to me. What did Socrates say? Death happens.

Across the bridge, into north Jersey.

I caught the driver looking at me. He quickly turned his eyes away from the rearview mirror, but it was too late. He was wondering about me just as I wondered about him. Why was he driving so fast? Why was the car armored?

We had been driving for nearly forty minutes when the car suddenly slowed. We were going through a small town at daybreak. We passed a park that had to be the town's center, and I peered out the window.

"Morristown," the driver said. "We're almost there."

Ten minutes later we stopped. There was a gate, a long driveway, a large house. The driver got out and took my bag. I followed.

Javier met us at the door. He smiled what I thought had to be a practiced greeting.

"I hope you're not too tired," he said. "We have our first session at nine. Someone will bring breakfast to your room in thirty minutes. Are you tea or coffee?"

"Tea," I lied. Why tea? I loved coffee in the mornings, but I wanted to fit in so bad, I was guessing what to say.

The Asian driver took me to a room and put my bag in front of the door. He bowed slightly, then walked away.

The room was set up for guests. There was a desk, a chest of drawers, a closet, a table, and a bed. Another door opened onto a bathroom. On the chest of drawers was a tablet.

I didn't know what to do, so I just sat on the bed. I thought of calling Mrs. Rosario and telling her that I had arrived safely, but I didn't know if I was safe or not. I looked at the time. Fourteen minutes past six.

Then there was breakfast. A black woman brought in eggs, fruit, toast, potatoes, and little packets of cereal. There was also a container of milk and a pot of hot water with a small box of tea bags. The box smelled of cedar. Nice. The black woman smiled at me, and I was grateful for her smile.

I turned on the tablet and watched the morning news. A man went berserk in Iowa. The New Jersey Devils won a hockey game in overtime. A starlet claimed to be pregnant by a man she had never met. Sweet.

Ten minutes to nine. There was a knock on the door, and when I answered it, I saw Javier in his wheelchair. He was going to show me to the room.

In the conference room. There were several young people sitting around a long table, some talking to each other, none of them looking my way for the moment. It was a micro version of Leonardo da Vinci's *Last Supper*. Michael wasn't there. I didn't want to look at the others, and so I drew triangles on the blank yellow pad on the table in front of me. The quietness of the group freaked me out. I wasn't liking this.

After a long while, maybe ten minutes in which nobody said a word to me, the door opened and Michael came in. He was dressed all in black. Tight pants, tight jacket, a pale-blue shirt that might have been silk, silver bangles. He was taller than I'd thought he was. Maybe six feet, maybe an inch or so more. Nice package.

"Some of you have already met," he said. "Others haven't. Let's go around the table and give our names. Then I'll do a short talk and we can go from there. Nobody has to do anything, even give your name. Everything is voluntary here. I hope we can pull off something good. I'm Michael Gullickson."

"Javier Gregory." Javier lifted a pale white hand in greeting.

"Tristan Braun." White; low guttural voice.

"Anja Marlena!" Round face, friendly.

"Drego Small." Black. Street.

"Mei-Mei. Mei-Mei Lum." She looked like a porcelain doll.

"Dahlia Grillo," I said, surprised at how loud my voice came out.

"As I've said before, we all know what is going on in the world." Michael sat as he spoke. "The C-8 companies are capturing, or at least controlling, all the major resources. In effect, they control everything we do, everything we eat, every place we go. Nobody thinks it's good.

Nobody thinks it's fair, nobody thinks it's going to get better.

"There are small groups all over the world willing to try to bring back a sense of normalcy to life. In Russia they call themselves the October Crew—something like that; in France they call themselves the Musketeers. In Britain it's the Eton Group, and they're the ones who are calling the conference in London to see what can be done to change things. I want to put together a group of people—you're sitting around the table now—that I think about—vaguely—as the Resistance.

"I don't know if we'll make a difference. But I know somebody has to try. So what I want to do is to go to London and listen in on the conference the Brits are having and see if we fit into their plans to resist C-8, and if we can make a plan to help our own cause. I think we should go and listen to the Brits, and then determine what we want to do."

"Working with the British group?" the black guy asked.

"Or without them," Michael said.

"We have our own problems to deal with." The white guy with the deep voice. "Why are we checking out Europe?"

"We're dealing with a number of factions with their own interests and problems," Michael said, "including C-8. The way I see it, they can all be against us or we can hook up with other groups when we think that'll work. We gotta play it by ear until we figure out our best moves."

"So when are we going to England?" Tristan.

"Tomorrow night," Javier said. "And there's another

thing. The C-8 group thinks of itself as neutral, not hostile. But that doesn't stop them from buying information, and it doesn't stop anybody from trying to get information to sell them. So we can expect spies in London. We can expect to be watched."

"I can't see any physical danger," Michael said. "They'll just be nosing around. Trying to figure out what we're up to."

"They won't get much if we don't know what we're up to," the black guy said. "It seems to me that we're flying blind."

"We don't have to fly completely blind if we make agent-based computer models," I said. "We'll know what we have, organize our database, and try to figure out what C-8 is looking for. Then we can use the information to model all the groups in the States and start formulating a plan."

"That doesn't make any sense." I looked over to where the Asian girl was talking with her head to one side. "If we *knew* what C-8 was looking for, we wouldn't need to go to London."

"We know that they're expanding in an economic world they've created. If anybody grows, it's because someone else somewhere is losing. So since we know their past history, and we have an idea about how the other groups around the world react to them, we can create a model," I said. "As we learn more, we'll make the models better."

"And that's suddenly going to predict what their intentions are?" she asked. "I don't think so. They avoid obvious patterns."

"Then I can factor that in," I said. "Thanks for reminding me."

Her coal-dark eyes never seemed to blink. Her face, smooth and white and circled by a carefully styled bob, made her look more like a decoration than a person. She stared at me, and I forced myself to stare back. I saw her fingers were on the black guy's forearm.

"Get some rest today," said Michael. "There's information on the computers in your rooms you might or might not want to use. There are also profiles of the members of the group, but don't make too much of them. We're going to have to learn about each other as we go along. But one thing I hope is that we can get to trusting one another as soon as possible. I trust all of you. I hope all of you can trust me."

I felt tense as I picked up the yellow pad in front of me. I thought the Asian girl was challenging me. I didn't like it.

In the room. There was a basket of fruit and two bottles of water on my table. Good, but where was the money coming from? I was still upset with the girl for saying my computer models didn't make any sense. I remembered Michael saying that there were profiles on the computer. I turned it on. I navigated through some game apps, then found the profiles. They were listed as "one time only" apps that would be erased once I went through them. "People grow as they question what they are doing and who they are," Michael had said at the meeting after mentioning the profiles. "We examine our lives and prosper."

There was a microwave and a small cabinet over the sink in the room, and I looked through both. The fridge had a pint of milk and some cheese. The cabinet had some crackers. I laid out some of the fruit and the crackers and the cheese on a plate and took it to the bed. Then I clicked on the profiles.

The first profile was Michael's. Naturally.

Dark screen, then a guitar wailing as if it were a crazy chick screaming. It played louder and louder, a deep bluesy sound; it softened and another voice came up. Then the image of a dude in a leather jacket facing away from the camera. I knew who it was right away.

I'm sailing to the edge of the Uni-verse
I'm scratching for love out there
I'm grabbing the souls of all my children
And anyone who cares

Oh, oh, oh-oh yeah!

It was Michael, and he sounded gravelly and funky. His face was white as anything, and his streaked hair and lined eyes made him look like something invented, but his voice was cool-strange, as if it was coming from another place altogether.

Then his image was covered up by a shot of a storm at sea. There were fragments of wood floating—perhaps a boat had capsized. The guitar kept getting wilder, and it sounded as if there was somebody crying in the storm. A headline flashed:

Plato's Cave Sold Out!

I knew the group, but I had never seen them live and hadn't really gotten into Michael. It was the band that had been swinging. They must have sold a million downloads every time they put out a jam. And I couldn't think of them as ever doing anything in the Real World. No way. But here was Michael, wailing away on guitar and calling up the blues like they went to school together or something.

Then Michael was looking into the camera, saying something like "times have changed" and the world was calling.

"We've been seduced," he said. "Seduced into our own little comfort zones, into our own little fantasies, and away from self-examination, from nation examination. We have to unseduce ourselves. It's as simple as that."

> *I'm sailing to the edge of the Uni-verse*
> *Leavin' all my thoughts behind*
> *Wrapped in gauze and tinsel paper*
> *In the black hole of my mind*

The music went on for another full two minutes and then stopped. It was some deep theatrical crap, but it was effective.

This was a Michael behind the Michael I saw. He was strutting as something special, and I was believing it.

The screen went dark for about thirty seconds, and I was just about ready to see if something had gone wrong when a shot of Javier's face came up. He was smiling.

"Well, this is my résumé and I hope to get into Yale Law School. My name is Javier Gregory and I live in Morris Plains, New Jersey. I attended St. Peter's Prep in Jersey City although I'm Jewish, and then Princeton. My folks are rich, so I won't need a scholarship. I hope that helps.

"My GPA is competitive and I've done some extra-curricular stuff that's typical of someone who is bright enough but also confined to a wheelchair. The good stuff I've done is a series of articles on the legal strategies of the civil rights movement of the nineteen fifties and how they evolved and also how more students participated in that than in any other movement. I think the success of the movement was at least partially, perhaps even mainly, due to the involvement of young people.

"I also have published a number of articles in law journals around the country, mostly historical surveys examining the legal crusades that helped to shape the nation as we know it.

"I played hockey in high school and during my first year at Princeton. A drunk driver on Route 287 ended my athletic career and left me wheelchair-bound. I do have some residual bitterness.

"Yale is my first choice because I'm excited about meeting the kinds of students that the university attracts.

Students, and the discussions they generate (hopefully it will be *we* generate), make Yale a special place to be.

"My long-term goals involve working toward a justice system that is blind to individual desires, a truly justice-based system with fairness for everyone. I am not sure that this is possible, but I am absolutely certain that it is worth working toward.

"I consider myself a decent human being and think of decency as an important trait. If accepted into Yale, I will do my best to make the school proud of my future accomplishments.

"Adding that my father, David Gregory, is a member of the Alumni Board of Governors is something I am hesitant to do, but it seems pretentious not to do so. Thank you for your attention and consideration."

Good résumé. I would have let him into Yale.

The next profile started out with an image of a big-headed white dude. He looked to be about fifty years old, maybe even older. There was an array of mikes in front of him, and you could tell it was some sort of press conference.

"I don't think we should—can everybody hear me?—I don't think we should get too happy with this situation. This Small kid—he's not small, but that's his name— Drego Small. I don't know what kind of name Drego is either, or even if that's his real name. A lot of these people have made-up names. I don't know why. That's just what they do. Anyway, the mayor—Mayor Andrikson—is all excited about this kid because he's stopping the fighting between the Miracle Mile Gang and the 187 First Gang, and that's supposed to make Chicago a safer place. Okay, on the face of it, it all looks good, but you got to ask yourself how he did it. The Chicago Police Department's gang unit couldn't stop those people from shooting each other every day and they're experts. Then all of a sudden this kid shows up—how old is he, fifteen or sixteen or something? And he stops the fighting.

"I see that this kid has both of these gangs listening to him, but I would like to know what he is telling them behind closed doors. Because I tell you this: if he can get these people to stop shooting each other, even for a weekend, he's saying something or doing something that's got a lot of power to it. And let me say this: I've seen his rap sheet, and he ain't no Gandhi or no Martin Luther King. This is a slick guy who's beaten some heavy charges. I'm willing to follow the mayor's line and give this guy some slack, but I think we shouldn't trust him until we make sure he's legit. Any questions?

"Would it have made a difference to me if he was white? Race ain't got nothing to do with this. The safety of people living in Chicago is the only thing on my mind. I'm asking myself the same questions every cop in the city is asking. Who is this guy? You don't see nobody walking on water and then you see this guy dancing across the waves. He don't look like Jesus to me. That's all I'm saying.

"Yeah, I'm afraid of his power. No, let me put that differently. I'm damned afraid of his power. There are about a hundred and fifty thousand gangbangers in Chicago and maybe that many and a half more guns floating around. We got fourteen thousand cops on the force. So we're outnumbered ten to one, outgunned, and I hope this kid isn't outmaneuvering us. I'm not kidding about this either. If my sister came on like this Drego does, I'd be afraid of her. This is a street guy with a lot of power. I'm asking the mayor to keep an open mind. That's it. An open mind."

A picture of Drego. It was a mug shot. He looked young. There was a picture of Drego in a prison jumpsuit. He had his hard pose on. Under it was his record. Attempted murder, attempted murder, kidnapping, RICO violation, possession of stolen goods.

I wondered how the hell Michael had ever hooked up with him.

The next profile started with a beefy-looking dude standing in front of a group of younger men who could have been soldiers or college guys.

"The difference between show-off push-ups and the real thing is that there aren't any gimmicks to a real push-up. You keep your body straight, you go down, you push up. You see these guys coming up and clapping their hands in front of their chests. That's bullshit, because when you do that, you're relaxing on the way down. You see some guys putting their feet on a locker or chair. But they only do ten or fifteen push-ups, and then they switch to some other sort of show-off stunt. As your physical instructor, what

I'm going to do here at the academy is work on getting each of you to do fifty strong push-ups. That'll get you five points on the FBI test and pass you on the SEAL screening test. In other words . . ."

There was a guy walking out in front of the group, about ten yards behind the guy speaking. A name scrolled across the top of the screen. *Tristan Braun . . . Tristan Braun . . . Tristan Braun.*

"What can I do for you, mister?" the instructor asked Tristan.

Tristan didn't answer. He took his shirt off and got down into the push-up position.

"We have clowns here the same way we have them everyplace else." The instructor addressed the guys he had been talking to as Tristan began doing push-ups.

As the instructor kept talking about pacing yourself, the attention of the students—I guessed they were students—kept switching back to Tristan. Then the instructor pointed to Tristan too.

"How many has he done?"

"Twenty!"

"He's a show-off, which means his head is halfway up his ass even before he starts," the instructor said. "That's not the way to physical fitness."

There was a close-up of Tristan doing push-ups.

"Thirty!"

The instructor looked at his watch, and the camera went to a clock on the wall.

"Forty!"

I watched as Tristan did one hundred push-ups in just

under two minutes. Then he stood up, wiped his hands, and walked away.

He was a show-off. I didn't think I liked him at all.

I saw a shot of a circle of cinder-block-and-wood huts. There were a few black women between the huts. They were tall, thin, with small breasts. They moved gracefully. A camera crew gathered outside one of the huts. It was badly staged. Out popped a young white girl. She was smiling. I think she was embarrassed, but her smile touched me.

"Hello, I'm Anja Marlena," she said. "We are in Zomba, Malawi. I came here six months ago to help clean up a site that, I guess, failed. It was an NGO—nongovernmental organization—site dedicated to helping the people of Zomba organize their economic lives and make a kind of progress. A team of small-village specialists, trained at Stanford and backed by the university, was going to teach their organizational skills to the people of Zomba and try to create a kind of model village."

From the same hut, a black woman emerged. She was taller than Anja and glanced at her with interest. Anja, without looking at the taller woman, slipped her arm around the slender waist and left it there as she continued.

"The modeling didn't particularly work out and the funding dried up. So everyone went home, and later me and two workmen came to reclaim the copy machines and fertilizer, but mostly we didn't want to leave anything behind that would embarrass the NGO.

"So we got here and one of the guys I came with got sick

and had to leave right away. He took a minibus up M-3, which is really just a dirt road, and then hooked up with some other people to get back to wherever he could get a plane to Egypt. That left me and a guy named John to gather up everything.

"It didn't look like we were making a lot of progress at first but the people helped us. Mostly, the kids helped us. Then one day John was gone. He just split. I knew he was going. I could feel it, so it didn't upset me too much. Some of the women told me that they could arrange for me to leave on a bus that came the following Thursday. My friend here, Cheza, let me move in with her instead of sleeping by myself in the school building. I didn't much know what to do, so I thought I would help her with the cooking. That amused her, and she called all her women friends over to watch me cook. They started teaching me to cook. Cassava, sweet potatoes, lots of rice, and sometimes chicken."

"She cooks like an English girl, but she sees like an African," Cheza said. "She sees with her heart."

"Then I started helping out at the primary school. The books are old and they don't have many, but the children want to learn. The children taught me ring games.

"Half of why I was doing this was because the place is so beautiful. You don't ever expect to be in a place this beautiful. You look into the distance and it gets hard to breathe. You look around you, at the people's faces, and you want to touch them because they are so sweet. That is a good word for the people in Zomba, sweet. Isn't that right, Cheza?"

Cheza shrugged and kind of grunted.

"What I don't like is the outhouses," Anja went on.

"Nasty. That's what they need—more than organizational help. Some indoor plumbing would make this the best place in the world. Or at least okay. When I get back to the States, I'm going to recommend just sending plumbing supplies. If the men don't know how to fix up toilets, the women will learn and teach them."

"You have to be good to her because she sees right through you!" Cheza said. "Maybe she was born with a veil over her eyes. They say some people born that way can see mysterious things."

The next profile started oddly. There was an Indian-looking man sitting and staring down. I couldn't see what he was staring at because the camera just stayed on his face. Every once in a while there would be a movement, an eyebrow would go up, or there would be a twitch in the corner of his mouth. It went on for a long time before I looked at the clock in the corner of the screen. The camera stayed on the guy for another two minutes as I wondered who he was.

He looked up and quickly down again, then shook his head, and the camera followed his hand down to a chessboard. He took one brown finger and knocked over a piece. Then he stood up and walked quickly away.

The camera moved around to the other side of the board. There was a young girl who sat there. It was the Asian girl from the meeting, Mei-Mei, the one who sat next to the black guy, Drego. Someone was pushing a microphone in front of her face and asking her questions.

"This is the third tournament you have won this year,"

the interviewer said as a caption in Chinese scrolled across the bottom of the screen. "How does it make you feel to win a tournament of this magnitude?"

"All tournaments have their interesting aspects," Mei-Mei said.

"Your rating is 2515, which is phenomenal in the chess world. How old are you?"

"Fourteen."

"Do you have ambitions to become the top female player in the world?"

No answer. Just the dark eyes looking at the interviewer, boring into him.

"Do you think you can compete with men on an international level?" The interviewer was trying to back off.

Mei-Mei didn't let him. She stared at him until the camera went away and the screen was full of Chinese characters. I wished I could read Chinese.

I thought her profile was finished, but the screen lit up again and it was Mei-Mei from the waist up. She looked about the same as she had at the meeting. This time she was sitting at what looked like a teak desk. On the desk there was a green box. Either jade or plastic.

"I'm called Mei-Mei Lum. My real name is Lum Mei Lan. I play chess and go. I like games because I like to win. That is about all that you need to know about me."

Then she opened the box and took out three black rings and put them on the fingers of her left hand. She held them briefly up for the camera to see, and then the screen went dark.

What the hell was that about?

The screen was dark for twenty seconds, perhaps a minute. Then it lit up and there was a bunch of kids sitting in what looked like an auditorium. The camera panned the kids, lifted to some more kids on the stage, and then stopped at a little girl. The same hair, the same face, but my eyes looked like pasted-on doll's eyes. They were so big. Where did they get the tape? It had been made over six years ago, when I was in the sixth grade.

It was funny, in a way, but it also made me want to cry. I was explaining to the kids, and the judges, how to go about measuring the height of a pyramid. It was simple triangles-and-shadows stuff, but I looked so earnest. I watched myself, the child me, and the tears started coming. I had believed that math was the key to everything. Just get the right numbers and the world made sense.

My nails looked awful, chipped and uneven from staying up all night chewing on them. My dress had a stiffly starched collar that flared out and made my face look pointy. I wanted the video to go on forever, to show how I felt when I was given the gold certificate laminated on a dark mahogany board. It didn't, of course. Little Dahlia faded to black. Gone. Forever.

I was lying on the bed, sniffling myself to sleep. In my mind, a little girl sat at home in a corner doing math problems from a workbook. When she was finished with each problem, she carefully checked the answer in the back of the book. She was so pleased when her answers were correct. She felt so safe, so secure. Nothing was wrong in her life. She had figured there were answers to everything, and knew she could find those answers.

There was a knock on the door. *Go away.*

Another knock. I wiped my eyes, looked at myself in the mirror, and then ran a wet cloth over my face. My smile felt lopsided as I opened the door.

"Is everything okay?" Michael.

"Sure, why not?"

He took a step backward, started to turn.

"Michael, why are you here?" I asked, keeping my voice to barely above a whisper.

"I live here," he said.

"You know what I mean," I answered. "Why are you *here*, in this place, in this time, in this fight?"

Standing in the doorway, his shoulders at an angle to the wood-framed rectangle, he seemed bigger. His eyes moved around the room as I moved away from the door. He didn't come in.

"Short version," he said. He was uncomfortable. "While I was out fronting the band, my folks were doing their thing. My dad ran a business, maybe two or three. He was making sportswear for a number of labels. They were making the clothes in Bangladesh. There were some headlines, a disturbance, and my father decided to close one of the businesses for a while. My mother wanted to go see the factory, to see if it really used kids to make the clothes."

He shifted his position.

"Come in," I said.

"No." He shook his head. "Anyway, against my father's wishes, she booked a trip to Bangladesh and went to see the factory. There was a street protest—she texted me; the *New York Times* called it a riot—and she was killed. The State Department hushed it up. My father lost it. I had never thought of them as being close, but I guess they were. He lasted three months and then killed himself. Over her, not the factory. Not the kids.

"I thought about who my mother had been, and who I was. She was somebody who *wanted* to see truth wherever it was. Who insisted on seeing even when she knew it was dangerous. I was somebody who hadn't seen or even known about the factory, who wasn't concerned about it, who didn't give a damn about anything except the brilliance of the stage lights. For the first time in my life, I was alone, with tons of cash, and this place, and stocks and accounts I haven't even added up yet, but I was alone. Onstage I'm usually alone in my head, but I always had a band, and crews and roadies and agents behind me. I swore there would never be another time when I would ever walk around in the daylight and not see. I want to see everything, Dahlia. I want to be responsible for everything I see."

"That's kind of heavy," I said.

"It's all light if you don't follow it up," Michael said, backing away.

I couldn't think of anything cool to say, so I just smiled and waved.

6

We packed for London. Michael told us not to forget to take the patches off our chips.

In 2016, the government had started a program in which every parent with a child born in America had the option of having a passport chip implanted in the child's right hip at birth. They said it would enhance national security and speed us through airports. It had seemed controversial at the time, but a lot of people went along with it. Then it got to be even more controversial when police departments started using the chips to track suspects. Some companies came out with chip covers, little screens that covered the area where your chip was implanted so it couldn't be traced by satellite. Some people had their chips taken out.

I had mine covered with two patches—one was the conventional blocking patch and the other was a titanium diffuser just in case somebody hacked the block. It was a little paranoid, but I didn't want people in my business.

I was excited about going to London. The computer had a lot of cool apps, and I was going to transfer them to my laptop, but then I saw that the computer also had a holographic projector switch. Right away, it came to me that if I could do computer projections in holographic mode, I could get a faster read than in flat mode. I packed both computers and told Michael what I was doing.

"You take what you need," he said. "If you need more stuff, we'll get it for you."

He smiled. I couldn't get a smile going because I was thinking really hard. When my brain is in gear, the smile doesn't get out too easily. Some people think I'm hard. I'm not. Maybe a little too intense at times, but not really hard.

Breakfast: eggs, juice, tea, coffee, cereal, fruit, toast, sausages, and something that looked like creamed spinach. Mei-Mei was sitting next to Drego again. She kind of leaned toward him, claiming part of his space.

Tristan was at the end of the table. He was eating the fruit and the spinach-looking stuff and staring down at his plate as Javier talked.

"It's a three-hour-and-fifteen-minute flight from Newark to Heathrow," he said. "So we should be there by seven at the latest. The British group is going to meet us and transport us to our hotel. From what we feel—feel more than know—the Eton Group doesn't really trust anyone.

They're talking about Anglo-American ties, but they've been burned in the past. Two years ago, they organized an Occupy rally in Parliament Square and there were more police than occupiers. Then all the leaders of the group were singled out and photographed. The police knew when they were coming, and who the leaders were."

"In England, they have those cameras everywhere." Tristan spoke without looking up. "You can't take a crap in London without being photographed."

"We aren't doing anything illegal," Javier went on. "We're just gathering information. We'll be photographed, but most likely, any information they gather will stay in Britain. They just gather so much of it."

"If the British have to watch everyone so closely," Mei-Mei said, "why should we trust them?"

"We'll trust them until we find a reason not to trust them," Michael said. "Our mission isn't to take over anything or even to occupy anything. We're living in a world where the stick seems to have nothing but shitty ends. We're looking to see if we can make a difference. Too many people are sitting by the roadside, too tired to move on. Maybe they're too old and tired. Maybe we are too. I have to know, one way or the other."

He looked away, as if what he was saying had affected him, but I didn't see how it had. He was still being a mystery.

It was a different world and I wasn't sure of myself. Everything about Michael and Javier smelled of bigger money than I had ever smelled. Even the way they sat at the table, so relaxed, so sure of themselves, said that this was where they belonged, and that they had been here before.

Tristan was alone with his thoughts and seemed almost as if he was brooding about something. Anja was light, airy. She tried talking to Tristan a couple of times, but he only grunted in return. Mei-Mei and Drego acted as if they were hanging out. I wondered how close they really were.

That left me. I had a feeling in the pit of my stomach that I was overmatched. When you got down to it, nobody was giving shout-outs to math. They all had something special going on, and I didn't feel as if I could keep up with them.

On the way to the airport, I was thinking of the invasion of Normandy. A bunch of guys thinking they were going to save the world and dying on the beaches.

Security. People going through while scanners were going over their chips. An Indian family tried to go through and the scanners couldn't read the woman's chip. The guards pulled her over to the side and had her stand against the wall while her children cried. Gross.

I got to the security kiosk, and the security dude ran the scanning wand over my right hip. My picture appeared on the screen next to him, and he looked at it and at me.

"Nice picture," he said. There was a map of my home area with code numbers next to it, which I imagined told him something about what group I belonged to.

"You're travelling with a band?" he asked next. "What do you play?"

"I sing."

"Oh? Sing something for me."

"No."

"Gotta pay to hear you, huh?" He grinned. His wand gave him the only power he had.

He waved me through and we went to the gate. Another check of our papers, another chip scan. Drego was pulled aside and Mei-Mei was told to move on. We entered the cabin, and found our seats in business class. The flight attendant started serving drinks, and nobody was talking about Drego. Mei-Mei took her seat, but she was looking anxiously toward the door.

Anja was doing a crossword puzzle. I bet she was nervous. Good. I wasn't the only one.

I'd flown plenty of times, mostly to Santo Domingo. The flight was three hours, about the same as our flight to London. Then it would take me hours to get to my relatives' home. Flying didn't bother me as much as going someplace and not being sure of what I was doing. I thought of Mrs. Rosario. Would I rather be home in the Bronx?

No. I was excited to be part of something. My palms were sweaty and I wanted to move on.

From the corner of my eye, I saw Mei-Mei shift position. I looked up and she was looking out the window; then I saw Drego coming into the cabin.

"They give you a hard time?" I asked him.

"They had to check to see if I had any hidden truths in my hand luggage," he said. He sat next to Mei-Mei. Yep, something was definitely going on over there.

The first hour I downloaded the *Times* of London,

the *Guardian,* *Der Spiegel,* and *El Diario.* Michael and Javier mostly talked to each other. Tristan slept, and Mei-Mei talked at Drego. Anja was watching a movie. I decided that she would be the one I would pal around with.

I fell asleep after an hour and woke up to the flight attendant telling me that we would be landing shortly and offering me a hot towel. For some reason I said yes, and she gave me a rolled-up towel that was too hot to do anything with. I saw Javier wiping his face with his, and so I did the same. It wasn't refreshing, and it didn't get my face that clean. It was just hot.

Customs at Heathrow meant walking through a screening device that looked like a metal detector. If they could pick up all your information just by having you walk between two sensors, it meant that they could find you anywhere by placing enough sensors around. I wondered if I should cover my chips again.

The Brits were waiting for us just outside the security area. They looked geeky and pale. My first thought was that they were probably super-bright kids. I also noticed that the girls were a little taller than the boys.

A van took us to the Chelsea Cloisters hotel on Sloane Avenue. It was one of those driverless things that worked okay, but I didn't like them because I was looking out the window thinking we were going to hit something. All the while, the Brits were talking about how glad they were that we had come over and how we were going to make a difference.

"The hands-across-the-sea thing really works, you know," a thin dude with big teeth said.

Anja nodded and smiled, and Michael reached over and shook the guy's hand.

At the hotel we got our key cards, and Javier said we'd be going to the first meeting at one o'clock the next afternoon.

My rooms were small, really just a teeny bedroom and a living room with a small stove, a few pots and pans, a countertop oven, and a kettle to boil water in. I started hanging up my stuff when Anja called. She said she was trying to get people to walk around the neighborhood but nobody wanted to go with her.

"I'll go," I said. "Maybe we can find some food."

We met in the lobby, and the clerk told us where the local grocery store was. Or, she said in her cool English accent, you could go out the back door and go to Marks & Spencer.

Anja had heard of Marks & Spencer, so we went there. On the way I told her how to translate the English money, pounds, to dollars in her head. All you had to do was figure that the pound was 10 percent more than the dollar.

We got to Marks & Spencer and it looked more like a clothing store. I couldn't believe the prices on the dresses and pants.

"But they are great!" Anja ran her hand over a skirt and watched the fabric seem to change color. It was a metallic material that caught the light and reflected whatever colors were in the light and also the ambient colors around it.

"These are nice," I said, "but check out the price! Does that say four hundred and twenty pounds?"

"You could wear it with anything," Anja came back.

"If I spent that much on a skirt, I'd have to wear it with everything!" I said.

We looked at some blouses. The metallic thing was in. There were silver, gold, and sheer black blouses. What got me was that some of the black blouses were like a deep color with almost no shine, but when you turned the fabric slightly, a pattern of black on black appeared. Very nice. Very expensive. It was the States all over again, but concentrated. No poor people were going to come in here.

The food was in the back, and we spent fifteen minutes just looking to see what the differences were between an American market and a British market. Anja thought the Brits went in for more fresh food. I didn't think so.

"They just have more expensive stuff," I said. "At least in this store. But Javier said not to worry about how much we spent when he was passing out the pounds."

I bought a lot of fruit and fresh veggies, and Anja bought some things with weird British names. She showed me a dessert called spotted dick.

"Anja, you are like a child," I said.

"I don't care," she replied. "But I'm not coming all the way to England and not trying this. And . . . my fine little friend, did you see the way the Brits were checking us out on the way to the hotel?"

"Oh, my God, that was so funny," I said. "I didn't know you had noticed it—but you do notice a lot of things. They kept looking at Drego and Mei-Mei and *all of us*, really, as if we were some kind of freaks or something."

"They were checking us out pretty good," Anja said. "But we are a different-looking group. They had one Indian boy with them, but the rest of them looked like they were cut out of the same batch of pizza dough."

Anja went on about how she didn't like the pep talk they were giving us even though she knew they were trying to figure out if we were serious or not. All the time she was talking, I was thinking how much I was getting to like her. Or at least I felt more relaxed around her. I didn't know why.

We got our stuff, got sniffed at by the woman monitoring the checkout counter, and made our way out the door into the busy London street.

"Dahlia, if you could be rich, I mean filthy, nasty, C-8 rich," Anja said, "and shop at Marks and Spencer every day, would you be tempted to chuck it all and sell your soul to the devil and give up the struggle?"

"No, I wouldn't," I said. "But maybe I'd consent to be rich for one day a week just to remember what I'm fighting against."

"Oh, I love a smart woman!" Anja said.

We walked back to the hotel—it was only like a ten-minute walk—with me remembering that I had forgotten to buy milk and Anja remembering she had forgotten tea.

Waiting for the elevator and watching some of the other

guests in the lobby. Since they could afford a London hotel, I guessed that when they were wherever they had come from, they saw the world through gates.

"What do you think of our little crew?" Anja asked.

"They seem sharp," I answered.

"You like Michael?"

"What does that mean?"

"The others you nail with your look—it's like you're penetrating them," Anja said. "Michael—you always kind of side-glance him."

"You like him?" I asked.

"Not like that," she replied.

"Not like *what*?"

"Dahlia, I didn't mean anything . . . honestly!"

"No problem," I said.

"Wednesdays?" she came back.

"Wednesdays what?"

"When we get filthy rich for one day a week"—Anja's smile widened—"we'll go shopping at Marks and Spencer on Wednesdays."

"You're on!"

As soon as I started cutting up the veggies I had bought, I realized how hungry I was. It was a residence hotel, and the small tuxedo kitchen was neatly tucked behind a sliding fabric-framed door. There was only one large skillet in the kitchen, but it was enough. I started sautéing some onions in garlic and margarine, and they filled the room up immediately with good smells. I added some mushrooms and carrots and turned the heat down.

I set up my computer, brought up the news, and saw that the reception was lousy. I switched to *boost* mode, and the picture came up but I lost the color. No big deal. The Tories were debating whether or not the government should take over the London *Times* as a cultural institution.

"No, because if you do, it won't be a cultural institution anymore, dummies!" I said aloud.

It really made me mad when things got screwed up in the same way all the time. Somebody was going to "save" something and ended up destroying it by making it into something it had never been intended to be. I threw some extra garlic into the pan in protest. I had bought thinly cut "chicken filets," and I sliced them up and stir-fried them into the other veggies. They looked like real chicken but they weren't real chicken. I knew a lot of people didn't eat them because they didn't know what they were. I didn't know what was in half the food I ate anymore. Nobody did.

I looked for a grater, couldn't find one, and diced up a few pieces of ginger as the guy who ran some theater talked about putting on a musical version of *Hamlet*. Sounded boring, and I was about to switch to another news outlet when there was a knock on the door. I opened it and saw Michael with a newspaper and a bag in his hand.

"I just wondered if everything was okay," he said.

"Yeah, I'm all good," I answered. "How are you doing?"

"Good. I went down the street and picked up a paper and a sandwich. I should have asked everyone first to see if they needed anything."

"What kind of sandwich you get?"

"Uh—it's kind of an egg salad sandwich," he said, holding it up so I could see it.

"It looks pathetic. You want something to eat?"

"You don't mind?"

I moved away from the door, and I thought he hesitated a second before coming in.

"Smells good, whatever it is," he said.

"It's just some veggies and fake chicken—you eat fake chicken?"

"Yeah."

"Sit down." I found the wooden spoon I had been using and pushed the veggies toward the center of the skillet. It did smell good now that the ginger was getting into the act. "Have you been to England a lot?"

"Not a lot, but a few times," Michael said. "We performed here at the Coliseum and in a few clubs in Brixton."

"What's leading a band about?" I asked.

"It's seriously together," Michael said. "If you're doing it right, you're bringing people together and they're creating something. You get the right people and you can see it happening. And if you're communicating, the audience sees it happening too. Then all you have to do is keep it going. You know what I mean? A lot of good things could happen in the world—*would* happen in the world—if people just weren't afraid of the momentum. The momentum builds and then somebody feels the need to stop it."

"Why?"

"Everybody is afraid of letting life get away from them,"

Michael said. "I think it's like when people get old—not just years old but in the way they think—and they see young people flying on the momentum of just being young, they sometimes get all shook and crazy and want to bring things back to some kind of order. Life is getting away from them. They want to slow it down and box it up."

"That sounds right," I said. I poured some orange juice into the pan, turned up the heat, and waited as the flavors came together. "In the band, how do you know if you have the right people?"

Michael watched me take the pan off the stove and use the spoon to put half the food onto a plate. Then I took the other half for myself, gave him a fork and the salt shaker, and sat down.

"If you have the right people, it just works out," he said. He hesitated for a minute, looked at me and smiled, then dug his fork into some mushrooms. When he lifted his head again, his eyes moved around the room as if he was looking for something. "You don't always know if you have the right people, because you can't tell what people are like. Not really. I mean, you can guess, but . . ."

A shrug. His eyes were looking around the room but not really seeing anything, just moving, and I knew he was thinking. But *what*?

"You do computer models of groups," he said after a while. "But you don't really know who the people are, right?"

"You don't have to know who they are to know what they'll do," I said.

"Are you ever wrong?"

"A lot, but it doesn't make a difference," I answered. "Because if you do the model right, it means you've thought through everything carefully. That's half the battle."

"You've got carrot on your chin," he said.

"Thank you." I felt around, found the little piece of carrot, and took it off.

"Dahlia." Michael leaned forward. "The fewer people you have in a model, the less effective it is, right?"

"It depends on their connection with group thinking," I said. "If they're stuck with thinking as a group, it doesn't matter that much."

"Awesome," he said.

Silence. When he ate, he didn't make noises on his plate with his fork, as a Dominican man would have done. He ate quietly, his head mostly down. What the hell was he thinking? We were sitting at opposite ends of the small table. It was only three feet long, so we were pretty close. I kept my eyes on my plate. When he looked up, he was checking out the rest of my little apartment.

"I think this is going to work," he said after a while. "I'm eager to get to the first meeting tomorrow. What do you think?"

"I'll tell you after I leave the meeting."

At the door. That little smile again.

Me: "See you later."

Michael: "You look good with carrot on your chin."

I was embarrassed.

He left and I looked at myself in the mirror. Not bad. Even without the carrot.

It was a twenty-five-minute ride to Dulwich College in south London. A British girl, or she might have been Irish, with long red hair was driving the van. She drove like a freaking maniac, and I was hoping that somebody would suggest they put the thing on automatic. The grounds at Dulwich were large and spacious. We got out and walked into the building. There was a big boat in the lobby, and one of the Brits started explaining why it was there.

Then another door opened and a group of about fifty boys, sweaty, dressed in green sweatshirts and matching pants, came rushing through. They slowed when they saw us—I thought they were looking at Michael mostly—and just kind of milled about, filling the air with a kind of boy stink and noise that sounded like a bunch of puppies. They had long hair, which they busily pushed away from their faces. Then they were looking at the rest of us.

"Your fan club," I said to Michael.

A priest-looking dude came along and shooed the boys away, and then we were shown into a huge gorgeous room with brown paneled walls, crazy high ceilings, and chandeliers.

"This must be where they breed them," Anja whispered.

The room had rows of chairs facing the windows. A small platform was set up, and one of the Brits who had driven with us went to it. He introduced himself and said how sad he was to announce that five groups had canceled at the last minute.

"But those of us who are here will, I am sure, make up in spirit what we lack in numbers," he said. "What I hope we do today is meet one another, exchange ideas and contact information, and begin the process that profitably leads to synergy and results. All this with the certainty that our activities are being monitored. The presence of other groups in and around London suggests that there is also an attempt to minimize our activities. Yet we move on. And it is with this hope that I greet and welcome you to my alma mater, Dulwich College.

"The tablets you found on your seats will provide instantaneous translations of what is being said and also give you the opportunity to talk among yourselves. The motto of the Dulwich school in Singapore is 'Building bridges to the world.' What we hope we can do is build not only bridges, but roads, tunnels, and air paths to a better life for all this earth's people. Thank you."

There was a formal printed program. Anja opened it and found a brief description of the C-8 group.

"Nothing new here," she said.

I looked over the list.

An Ocean of Influence
The Eight Corporations That Threaten
What Remains of the Free World
COMPILED BY THE ETON GROUP

JENNINGS INTERNATIONAL
Started as a secret conservative think tank of billionaires after the reelection of U.S. President Barack Obama. Their policies

quickly switched from an advisory role to wielding their influence in the world's economic markets.

NATURAL FARMING

This former farm-subsidy advocate group quietly bought up food distributorships around the world and began to buy arable land in third world countries. The most aggressive of the Central Eight corporations. They also cornered the market on seed and grain patents and genetically engineered foods.

CLOUD COVER

This Hong Kong–based company dominates satellite placement and distribution, and thus worldwide Internet access.

CRYSTAL LAKE

A Euro Zone leader in water purification. Seemingly harmless until the world's water supply was drying up, then began vying with local governments for control of water assets.

SPORTS DIRECT

The world's biggest supplier of weaponry. Took full advantage of the 2017 NATO military cutbacks. Will supply cheap weapons until a war heats up.

CTI

The Cyto Technology Institute started off as a relatively small research foundation. It was seen as a good move when it expanded its operation to absorb other operations, but troubles soon developed when private investors looked to increase its profitability.

JEREMY FUND

This international monetary giant controls the flow of money throughout the world, ensuring that have-not countries are always on the brink of rebellion.

THE ANDOVER GROUP

The control of oil and fossil-fuel technology did not seem to be a threat in the growing age of nuclear and solar energy. The Andover Group was not only capable of using their quarter of the world's energy resources to enhance their own profits, but they were also able to control both nuclear and solar developers who utilized the older technologies in ancillary operations.

Anja was right, nothing new.

The greetings were first, and then there would be six delegations making presentations. Michael was speaking next to last.

The first speaker was a thin kid with rimless glasses. I didn't know many kids who wore glasses. He started his speech with his head back, saying something nobody could understand. I thought he was speaking a different language at first, and then I began to understand what he was saying.

"Theeeey aaaare eeeee-vil!" He kept saying it over and over again. Bullshit drama to the core.

Anja was two seats down from me and shaking her head. There was a space between us where Javier's wheelchair had been for a second or two before he wheeled off and got into a hush-hush conversation with one of the Brits.

Anja pointed to her tablet and I looked down at mine. She was texting me.

A: Everyone in C-8 believes in what they are doing. Sometimes they have to stop thinking for days at a time to keep their graspy hands reaching out, but they believe, girl, THEY BELIEVE!

Interesting. I had always thought of C-8 as evil people too. But if they did believe in what they were doing, thinking it was somehow right for them to be taking advantage of the weak or the ignorant or whoever they were standing on at the time, I knew it would be easier to build a model mapping out their behavior. True believers in money, like true believers in Heaven, or Hell, or anything, were wonderfully predictable.

Two Australians came up together and got into a long rap about how nobody could beat C-8 because they had all the weapons and all we had was our ideals. The Australians were true believers too.

When it got to be Michael's turn, I found myself tensing up. I wanted him to do well. It was like he was representing the guys from America, which was good, but there was more.

Michael hunched his shoulders and tapped the mike twice before beginning.

"I've never been in a shooting war where people scream and fall down in pain. The thought of it scares the hell out of me. But the war we're in, a war in which the enemy delivers shiny kitchen appliances to your front door, and in which they have rows and rows of frozen meals available in supermarkets, is a war nevertheless. We have simply skipped over the body counts. The term 'body count' started showing up seventy years ago in Vietnam. It sounded better than 'dead people,' so the papers and the after-action reports people used the phrase a lot.

"Then somebody, probably Americans, came up with the term 'collateral damage.' That meant people who were dead or wounded but not necessarily identified as the 'enemy.' That's the world we live in today; that's the war we are facing today. Huge companies bring marvelous gadgets to our lives and there is collateral damage. Perhaps a few thousand children dead in India, or an African village decimated, or a few hundred miners in West Virginia quietly coughing their lungs out.

"What we need to do is to start calling dead bodies by their rightful name: 'dead bodies.' If they get killed fighting for scraps of food in Detroit, or die waiting for medicines in China or Russia, we have to start seeing them.

"We can't continue to let the global corporate masters keep on pushing people to the edges of society and then condemn them as outsiders. We can't give in to the idea that the immorality of greed that is killing our planet is somehow all right if it can be justified in any small corner of the world. The enemy is already within the gates; they are among us, seducing us with their baubles and playthings, as they quietly take away our futures.

"I hope we will fight together for a clear day in which everyone sees every truth. Thank you."

There was a little applause, and then the Brits stood up and began to clap loudly, and some joy crept into the place.

Good, Michael. Damned good.

On the way back to central London. The Brits were chatty, talking about some messages they had received and reassuring us that the low turnout didn't mean anything. I was pleased, but I felt myself zoning out and knew I needed some serious sleep time.

An exchange of information at the hotel while the doorman, a big, beefy dude, looked on. The van was pulling away, and we all seemed tired as we went into the lobby.

"It's a promising start," Michael said.

"Promising?" Drego. "If you believe that shit, you're dumber than you look!"

We froze at the sudden tension of the out-of-the-blue put-down. I glanced over at Drego and saw his neck was puffed as if he was ready to leap at somebody. Behind him, just peering around his shoulder, was Mei-Mei, staring at Michael.

"Well, I think it was promising," Michael said softly.

Drego snorted and turned away. Mei-Mei didn't move; she just kept staring at Michael.

Drego got to the tiny elevators first and walked in. Mei-Mei *backed* in, still working that stare. The elevator held only four or five people, and Michael stepped in. He was face-to-face with Drego. I got in behind him, wondering what the hell was going on. Drego and Mei-Mei got off on the fourth floor, and when the door opened on the fifth, I asked Michael if he was okay.

"Yeah, I'm all good," he said. "I've been here before."

Where? I wondered.

Back in my room I fell across my bed, exhausted to the bone. There were parts of me completely wasted and aching and stiff that I wished I could just discard. Get a new body. Put the lights out. Pull the covers up. Fart in the darkness.

Me in the talk show of my mind:

"Drego thinks we should start making alliances," Mei-Mei was saying.

"Fuck Drego," I answered.

"If it comes to a showdown, we have to know who's got our backs," Mei-Mei said. "Who we can rely on."

"Apparently we can't rely on Drego," I said. I wanted to add "or you," but I didn't.

"I think Drego's right." Mei-Mei's voice in the darkness sounded ominous.

I fell asleep.

7

Sunday. Did we still have Sundays? Was somebody, somewhere, still washing themselves and getting ready to go to Mass? Were there mothers still twisting hair around curlers or ironing dresses so God wouldn't be embarrassed when we showed up late?

Anja called. Michael and Drego were shouting at each other on the fifth floor. She thought we should be there.

I looked in the mirror and saw a complete mess. There was some dried saliva on my cheek, and I grabbed a towel and wiped at it. I got my jeans on and padded, barefoot, out to the staircase. I could hear Drego shouting at Michael the moment I opened the fire door. Something about "manning up." They were in front of Michael's room.

Drego was standing, feet apart, in the middle of the hallway. Three tourists, perhaps a man and wife and their child, stood back and watched, wondering what the hell was going on, or if they should try to pass this black man, veins prominent in his neck as he vented in the narrow corridor.

"If you're going to be effective, you have to be ready for anything!" Drego looked fierce. Mei-Mei was a few steps behind him, flat against the wall. "You can walk into this with your eyes closed if you want, man, but anybody who can see knows you're scared to make a move! You just don't want to face the reality that's staring you in the damned face!"

"I'm going my way, Drego," Michael said calmly. "If you want to go a different way, then go. I certainly won't try to stop you."

"We're either together or we're not." Mei-Mei's voice sounded hoarse. "You said the biggest danger was self-destruction, that we would turn against each other. Now you're telling Drego he can go his own way. To me, Drego is the only one with balls in this crew."

"It doesn't take balls to scream in a hallway," Michael said.

"Bullshit!" This from Drego. "We could be dead by this time next year!"

"Or this time next week," Michael said. "If your life is that important to you, then run with it."

Drego put his shoulder against the wall and shook his head slowly. I looked at Mei-Mei, and she looked absolutely scary. The wide face seemed wider, rounder, the porcelain skin contrasting even more brilliantly against the dark-brown eyes. I saw that she had put mascara on her lashes, dark in front and green on the edges. One small hand, fingers spread, touched the gaudy paper on the wall. She looked like an animated doll. Beautiful. Fragile. Not really human.

Drego straightened up suddenly. He looked at Michael with contempt, then started walking away.

"Drego, Roderick has invited us out for food tonight," Michael called after him. "I'd like you to come."

Drego continued down the hall for a few steps, then stopped. He turned and looked at Michael. "Roderick of the Sturmers?"

"Yeah," Michael said. "The Brits said that a lot of people were showing up in London. The corporations are trying to make this whole conference look like some kind of freak show. And it figures they're going to be looking for us."

"Why you want to go eat with Roderick?" Drego. His voice was calmer.

"Roderick wants something—maybe just to figure out who we are. I don't know. But it's interesting that he's shown up here," Michael replied. "Maybe he's just doing a check on who's got balls. Midnight tonight. You coming?"

"Yeah, I'll be there."

I remembered seeing a story on the Sturmers online. The site was profiling neo-Nazi groups. They gave his real name as Jerry Rowland. The "Roderick" came from the last Visigoth king.

"There is a tsunami, a hurricane, interlaced with torna-does, rising from the bowels of the earth!" he had mum-bled in his "down-home" role as a good ol' boy who was "tired of being pushed around." "It is not God-made, but man-made. We are the storm. We are the Sturmers."

He wanted his message to strike fear in the heart of every-one who listened to him. Fool. People already knew that C-8 was running the show; what the hell did they have to fear from a bunch of misfits who called themselves the Sturmers?

What the Sturmers did to fit in was to act as mercenaries for anyone who would pay them enough to commit the vio-lence they did, or would pay them *not* to commit violence. To the Sturmers, and to Roderick in particular, there was no conflict except with those who opposed them. Roder-ick himself was a big guy, broad, and always in costume. Sometimes it was some country-western outfit, other times it was his biker mode. But always with enough Nazi decorations to show he was an asshole.

We were together in Michael's room talking about our dinner with the Sturmers. Anja texted me that we were doing too much talking. She was wrong. Drego wanted to know about Michael's endgame.

"To get a clue as to what Roderick will do," Michael said. "What is he trying to find out about us? Do the Sturmers have strengths we don't know about?"

"And you're going to get the straight scoop at one meet-ing?"

"With your help, with everybody's help, I'm going to

get as much information as I can," Michael said. "So will Roderick. He's not inviting me here because he likes my company."

"And if there's violence?"

"There won't be." Tristan spoke up. "There wouldn't be a meeting if he didn't need to find out how strong we are."

"How strong are we?" Mei-Mei asked.

"Stronger than you think," I heard myself saying.

Mei-Mei gave me a look that was like spitting on me. I wanted to kick her ass so bad, I could taste it.

"You all right?" Tristan asked Michael.

Drego had already left, and Mei-Mei had followed him. I knew they would be talking smack about Michael as soon as they left.

"Yeah, I'm okay," Michael said.

"You sure about this meeting with Roderick?" Anja asked. "I mean . . . he's known to be a sneaky SOB."

"I'm not sure, but I think I have to take the chance," Michael said. "I need good people with me. Drego's a hot-head, but he knows the changes."

"I guess." Tristan's voice had an edge to it that I liked.

When Michael asked me to stay a minute, I was glad. Then I panicked, because I thought he might hit on me. Men do that kind of thing when they're uptight, and I got the feeling he was getting uptight.

"Can you do a social model?" he asked. "Work Roderick into it, and maybe the Gaters as well. Everybody thinks there's something going on, and we're all looking at just the business side. But it could be something else."

"Like what?"

"If the Sturmers got a new weapon, for example. How would that make things different?" Michael asked.

"A new weapon?" I asked. "C-8 already has enough fire-power to keep us in line."

"Things are beginning to move," Michael said. "It's clearly not a coincidence that the other groups are showing up in London."

"You thinking something is going to go down over here?"

"No, or at least I hope not. The C-8 corporations are always watching for a chance to make a move. You know the Andover Group, and how they're controlling twenty percent of all the energy resources in the west?" Michael sat on the sofa, stretched his legs out before him and crossed them at the ankles. "The Brits are telling me that they're suddenly giving up their Nigerian oil interests."

"To whom?"

"The Nigerian government," Michael said. "That's too sweet for it not to be a cover-up, or a diversion. There's got to be something fishy about it."

"Michael, straight up, are you holding back some stuff we should know?" I asked. "Because when things stop making sense . . ."

"That's why the Brits are so worried," he answered.

"They coming with us tonight?"

"No," Michael said. "They want their own take on the situation."

I didn't like it, and I was feeling a little paranoid. I knew what C-8 was about, and I knew what life was becoming for everybody. But I wanted to either do something about the shit or go back to the Bronx. I didn't want to be a bump on anybody's road.

At eleven, we piled into a rented van, turned on the auto-GPS, and let the vehicle make its way through the streets of England's capital. Forty minutes later, we turned into a darkish street, the Kilburn High Road. On the left side, the Tricycle Theatre flashed a blue neon sign. Our meeting was taking place at the Black Lion.

You could hardly see "The Black Lion" printed above the windows. There were slatted blinds that shielded the interior from the public, and the heavy doors damped down the music. If you could call the crap that was blaring through the pub music. It sounded like golden oldie ska being played by a band of crackheads. The stupid *thump, thump, thump* of the bass alone was enough to make me want to leave.

The Sturmers were in their biker-cum-Viking outfits. Lots of black leather, silver studs, obscene tats, and bare arms. A big table had been put up along the wall, and I saw a huge, bearded clown waving us over the moment we came in. I figured that must be Roderick.

The whole set was carefully staged. I felt the hair on my neck stand up, and I needed to pee, only there was no way I was leaving my little group and going into a bathroom alone.

There were ten Sturmers. Six guys and four girls. They were making enough noise for twice that many.

My running talk show: I'm in the bedroom with Michael, and he talks to me about computer models while I sit on the bed in a half slip. Stupid, but sweet.

"Here comes the posse!" Roderick throws his arm around Michael's shoulder. "Let's get this party started!"

Roderick. Up close he has a huge nose with large pores. He's taller than he looked in the profile piece, maybe six feet six, a shaggy, uneven beard that is dyed red, bad teeth, and what look like acne scars. Disgusting. That's the way the papers say he wants to look. He wants people to feel uncomfortable and turn away. He catches my eye and smiles. His lips are greasy. I don't turn away.

A few stupid jokes from the Sturmers as we watch their girls swig down whatever it is they're drinking. Roderick signals the waitstaff, and they disappear into the kitchen for a minute and then come out with plates of food.

"What are the girls wearing?" Anja, under her breath.

"Slut strips!" I said.

The slut strip came in around twenty years ago and apparently was hot for a while. It was just a strip of aluminum covered by two microthin layers of silver. You could glue them onto walls or your knapsack and pick up the Internet. Girls put them on their lower backs, which was supposed to make some kind of statement. To me it was just a high-tech tramp stamp. Every time a Sturmer girl moved and her blouse went up, you could see her slut strip flash.

The food. Nothing special, just lots of it. The talk around the table was really stupid and really loud.

The Sturmers were mostly downing pints of dark beer

and shots of some clear liquid. I asked one of them what it was, and he said it was embalming fluid.

"Y'all got a nice smile, lady!" he says.

I flashed him a nicer smile, thinking all the time that his down-home drawl didn't cut it.

Nobody was talking about anything real, just a whole bunch of eating and drinking and feeling each other out. I don't like drinking, and the cloudy cider I'd been nursing was getting my stomach upset. The Sturmer women started floating around the table. Pierced faces, makeup thrown on if they were wearing any, tight jeans, and combat boots. Some of them were missing teeth. Any one of them looked like she could be a chapter in a freaking social worker text.

Mei-Mei nudged my elbow and pointed her nose toward a broad guy with long hair who was trying to get the waitress's attention. As he turned, I saw a sign painted on his jacket: "If You Can Read This, the Bitch Fell Off!" Hilarious. If he hadn't already noticed, all the Sturmer women looked as if they had fallen off something. Maybe a dump truck.

We ate and waited for Roderick to let us in on why we were at the Black Lion. My mind shifted back to the Andover Group's giving up the Nigerian oil rights. Whatever Andover had in mind was too sophisticated for the Sturmers. You got smart people like the ones they had in C-8, and you couldn't mix them with anybody like the Sturmers. They were going for two different things. C-8 was shooting for profits that the Sturmers couldn't even have imagined. The Sturmers would be happy with their next beer.

We ate, and waited, and then the punch line came. With Sturmers, the punch line was always violence.

Roderick reached over and started feeling up the waitress. She looked Irish. Tall, thin, kind of pale, and just fragile enough for somebody to want to take care of her. She pushed Roderick away as she cleared the end of the table..Grinning, he reached from behind and put a huge hand between her legs. A younger white guy who was busing tables stepped in and knocked Roderick's hand away.

"What the hell ya doing?" he yelled.

Roderick, mouth open as if he was surprised, looked the kid up and down and then laughed.

"Olga! He's yours."

A Sturmer chick stood, walked over to the guy, and punched him in the groin. The guy went over quickly, and she chopped him on the back of the neck. The Sturmers burst into laughter. Stage shit. It was all stage shit. I glanced over toward Tristan. Calm eyes. Such calm eyes.

A few of the other customers stood. You could see the fear in their eyes. They didn't know what was going down. This was the kind of world we were living in, and people like Roderick were gaming it to the max.

He stood up and raised his arms. All the Sturmers shut down. More theater shit. The reference to Nazis was clear, and they were milking it.

"We're disturbing the people," Roderick said. "There's another room. Maybe we can go to it."

"You grabbing any more women?" Mei-Mei asked.

"I wouldn't touch you, sweetheart." Roderick grinning. In charge. Big man. Drego's throat bulging with anger.

A bootlicking sucker, his fat gut hanging over his belt, showed us to another room. Tristan went in first. I followed him. He looked around, sat at the long dark-wood table. The tables were heavy, mahogany. Real wood. Roderick was chowing down on some kind of meat, holding the bone in his hands. The waiters brought the rest of the food from the outside tables.

If they're putting up with this, it means that they've been well paid. In the computer projections, I need to add a money trail.

Roderick stood and wiped his face with the back of his hand.

"Whatever is said, whatever anybody feels, there's something we all know," he said. "What we know is that some of us are better than others. We can play games about democracy or equality, but in our hearts we know. What I want to do is two things. Not very complex, not very risky, not very hard. One is to let everyone feel in their heart what I say aloud, which is the truth. That there are people on top and people on the bottom, and there always will be!

"Once we say this—and we all believe it; there are no fools here—then we can get to the next step. And that step is to make life better for everyone," Roderick went on. "What that better life is like we can question, but who doesn't want a better life, eh?"

The bone, the fat dripping off the glazed skin, partially

covered Roderick's face as he bit into it. I wondered what role Roderick could play in the C-8's latest plans. Maybe he was not as confident as he seemed if he still needed all the theatrics.

"How do you see us getting a better life, Roderick?" Michael asked.

"Hah, I'm glad you said 'us.'" Roderick wiped his mouth with his sleeve. "The trouble, as I see it, is that the crawly creatures are the biggest problem. They are the neediest, so it's natural that they invent wars against us to get what they want. But they hold the key to the way everybody has to live. You can't travel anywhere for fear that they'll attack. Yeah, I know what they want is food, and sometimes medicines. But they are still the source of the conflict, the root cause."

"And if we just found a way to give them more?" I asked.

"They would still want to be equals in an unequal world, wouldn't they? And please, don't bore me with some nonsense about us all groping our way to some level playing field. That ain't happening, baby."

"And you're proposing?" Michael.

"To control them," Roderick said. "To make the world a better place by removing the worst elements. If you have a diseased body, a cancer growing in you, you try to remove that cancer. You don't kill the body."

"A final solution?" Michael touched his fingertips together.

"Hey, would your women screw one of those guys from Peru?" a Sturmer chick asked. "One of those little greasy dudes? I don't think so. So what's going to happen is they're going to stay pissed and look for ways of getting what they want. You can't blame them, but you can sure as hell stop them."

"There's no reason to make a decision—any decision—tonight or even over the next few months," Roderick added. "It's just something to think about. We stop the wild kids, the ones roaming through the streets with Uzis and butchering people, and we raise the stock of the world and have more resources to pass around. You guys know who you are. You're top of the pile. You got more education, more class, and a pissload more brains than the average Gater, than half the people in C-8, than every jerk—what do they call them? *Favelos*? Tell me you don't know that. Tell me that Asian chick doesn't have an IQ as high as two of them put together."

"Bottom line, Roderick." Michael put his hands palm down on the table. "How do you plan to 'stop' these kids, these *favelos*?"

Roderick laughed. He looked at the Sturmers with him, and they chuckled to themselves knowingly.

"We'll find a way," he said. "Trust me."

"Why we meeting in London?" Drego. "Why not New York, or Boston?"

Roderick turned to Drego slowly.

"Y'all over here making friends, Othello." Roderick let the words slide out his mouth. "We just want to know if we gonna be among those friends. Now you can't blame a good old Southern boy for thinking on that, can you?"

Back to the eating and drinking. A Sturmer girl throwing kisses at Tristan. One of the Sturmer men sticking out his tongue at Mei-Mei.

Winding up. Michael asked for our bill, but the Sturmers, predictably, paid for it all. We shook hands all around on the sidewalk. The narrow street was dark, but not so dark we couldn't see Roderick relieving himself against the side of the building.

8

At the hotel. Michael was saying that we should start packing up to go home. He was collecting his mail, and I saw the clerk hand him a small leather pouch.

"Maybe just hang in London for a day or two and then split."

It sounded good to me, and I immediately started thinking of buying gifts for Mrs. Rosario and the old man. Mei-Mei was whispering something stupid to Drego. I couldn't hear it, but I knew it was stupid. Javier was already in the elevator when Michael called to him. There was an urgency in his voice, and we all stopped.

Drego caught the elevator door and Javier powered out. We all waited as Javier took the pouch and the paper that Michael handed him.

"This legit?" Michael asked Javier.

"Could be." Javier turned over the paper. "Let's call the Brits."

"What's up?" Tristan.

"This is a diplomatic pouch, and there's a message in it that's supposed to be from a Sayeed Ibn Zayad," Michael said.

"Who's that?" Tristan.

Michael shrugging. Everybody else too pooped to care.

Anja asked if she could come to my rooms.

"Sure."

"What did you think of tonight?" she asked when we got there, taking off her shoes. "It wasn't as stupid as it looked."

"What did you see that I didn't see?" I asked. "Because it looked stupid as hell to me."

"We come to London and the Brits are like looking at us to do something, and then the Sturmers invite us out to their little circus," Anja said. "They're feeling us out and the Brits are feeling us out—"

"You don't trust them?"

"They don't trust us," Anja said. "But why is everybody paying so much attention to us? We're a smart group, and we're all edgy—"

"I'm not edgy!"

Anja giggled. "D-girl, you are the edgiest person in the group. You're the one who's calling people out. Mei-Mei just follows Drego. Drego's got his ghetto cape on with the street-cred labels sewn on the outside. You're edgy, girl."

"Okay, now what?"

91

"You have any idea what we have that anybody wants?"

"Maybe they want to take you as a hostage," I started to kid.

Anja's face said she wasn't kidding. "What do you think?"

"Michael's got something going on?"

She shrugged.

Morning. Coffee in Michael's room. Everybody's there, along with Victor, who seemed to be able to speak with authority for the Brits, and a girl who said her name twice and I still couldn't understand it. Victor was talking.

"Sayeed Ibn Zayad is from North Africa. He mostly operates like a warlord in his country, terrorizing people much the way that your Sturmers do, but on a wider scale," he said. "We suspect he has some connection with C-8, but we're not sure what he's up to exactly. British intelligence knows that he's in the country, and that he has sent some people to the conference. They don't want us anywhere near him."

"You're dealing with British intelligence?" Tristan.

"It's more a case of them dealing with us," Victor said. "It would be an embarrassment to the government to have any formal connection with what amounts to a terrorist group."

"You could have told us about British intelligence," Michael said. "And I don't know anything about this guy. Where did you say he was from?"

"Morocco. But he has some influence in the Iberian Peninsula as well," Victor said.

"I still don't know that much about him," Michael said.

"It's the American disease," Victor said. "To you people, history begins in Boston and ends in San Francisco."

"That's nonsense." Michael waved Victor off.

"Michael, you won the bloody Second World War too, and you don't know anything about that either!" Victor said.

"Yeah, and the Revolutionary War too," Michael said.

I looked at Anja, and her eyes were huge. We were all feeling a little stupid.

"So what's up with this guy now?" Michael asked.

"He's making bolder and bolder moves," Victor said. "When he was in the mountains outside Marrakech, he devoted most of his time just to screwing up the tourist trade and supporting some incredibly stupid pirates around Gibraltar. He was more of a nuisance than anything else.

"But now he's out of the mountains, heavily armed, and flaunting his power. The question is whether or not he has any new power, any backing that's not obvious, or whether he's just falling in love with himself as every other tyrant has done in the past."

"So how are you going to find out? Do you have spies?"

"We sent in an eighteen-year-old from Surrey, a very clever boy with golden-brown skin and startling green eyes," Victor said. "Somehow they found him out and sent us his eyes in a small ivory case."

"So now what, you gave up on him?" Tristan.

"I don't give up that easily." Victor shook his head. "From Sayeed's letter, I see he's found you and wants to meet you. The word is that he didn't bring his people into Dulwich because of the weapons ban. That's probably eighty-five-percent bluff. Actually, I think he wants us to be impressed by his weapons. But if he's here, he's here for a reason. I think maybe your little group can find out. He's not going to try to intimidate you."

"We're Americans . . . so that means . . . ?"

"Let's face it, Michael, you are the most violent people on the planet. You can't seriously deny that."

"The Sturmers tried to intimidate us," Anja said.

"You held your own against them," Victor said flatly.

"You got spies everywhere?" Drego.

"In this country," Victor said, "we have eyes."

"So what do you want us to do with this . . . ?"

"Sayeed Ibn Zayad. You'll have a dossier by tonight. What I want you to do, if you find the scheme appealing, is to answer his letter. By now, everybody knows you met with the Sturmers. Meet with Sayeed, too. In the end he might not show up, but it's worth a try. Whatever we can find out has to be useful."

"If that was your intention all along, why didn't you say it the first time we met?"

"It wasn't my intention at all," Victor said. "But beneath the bluster and speeches at the conference, I sensed that some people are at least taking us seriously."

"Why don't you just clear it with British intelligence and go yourself?" Drego asked. "If you're as stiff-upper-lippish as all that, why don't you just contact this Sayeed and invite him to tea?"

"Because I don't have the nerve to face down our national intelligence system, and I don't have the mystique of being American. And we're not led by a rock star such as Michael. Sayeed won't trust you, but he's going to want to see Michael up close. He's going to want to see the Americans up close. He might try to bluff his way through a meeting with you, but he is far more apt to reveal himself than he would in a meeting with us."

"Victor, I think you're playing pussy with us," Michael said. "And I don't like it. If we meet with Sayeed, I'll tweet you. Or maybe I won't."

9

Watched the news on television, then decided I needed to get some fruit to eat later. I had an itch on my thigh and stopped at a local pharmacy on the way to the store. After I spent ten minutes explaining to a pharmacist who spoke in what I thought was a Middle Eastern accent, he told me he couldn't help me unless he saw the area. I think he wanted me to take my pants down in the shop. I said no, and then he gave me a tube of some cream. I hoped it would work.

My leg itched. The rooms seemed drearier than before. The elements were coming together, but I was feeling frustrated. Maybe C-8 was counting on that. I just knew I wanted to go home.

In Michael's room with the whole crew. Drego asked Michael if he was going to meet with Sayeed.

"What do you think?" Michael asked. "If he pulls the same crap as the Sturmers did, it won't be of any use. If Victor is right, if we're getting respect just because we're Americans, then a meeting will give Sayeed a boost. Do we want that?"

"Michael, listen to me." Mei-Mei pulled up a chair and sat in front of Michael. "You don't have the nerve to face Sayeed! The bottom line is that you don't have the nerve! Sayeed will eat you! He'll eat you and spit you out like the boy you are!"

Mei-Mei's round head was inches from Michael as she vented her rage at him. I looked at her: the narrowed eyes, the mouth a red, bloodless wound stretched across the bottom of her face. Her small hands were clenched and pounded into the tops of her knees as she spoke.

"You were a joke at the meeting with the Sturmers! They were laughing at you! At us!"

I felt my heart beating faster. My throat went dry.

"That Sturmer girl would have kicked your ass, Michael! You would have been lying there on that floor sucking sawdust if she'd wanted you there! You are a punk!"

I felt myself reaching for Mei-Mei's hair.

I snatched it and ripped her away from Michael. Now I was in her face. She was shocked. I didn't know how I looked, or what anyone was thinking, but I knew I was pissed.

"Back off, Mei-Mei! Back off and give the people who

want this thing to work a chance!" I was screaming at her. "And do it now before I snap your doll's head off your pretty little body!"

Mei-Mei was shocked. The face went blank for a minute. Her hands came up to disentangle my fingers from her hair.

She was standing, moving away. Now stumbling. There were tears in her eyes. She wiped them away in a fury of motion.

"I am forever your enemy!" She spit the words at me. "Forever!"

"You and the common cold!" I was already sorry for what I was saying. But I couldn't stop myself. "Why don't you just grow up?"

She left the room and rushed into the hallway. There were tourists, stock-still, holding their breaths, wondering what was going on. Drego followed Mei-Mei into the hall.

"We're all tired," Tristan was saying. His voice was calm, steady. "Let's get some rest and start again later."

Someone was saying yes. We were all tired. Anja and Tristan went by me, and it was just me and Michael in the room. I was collapsing against the cream-colored wall, close to tears. Michael came over to me and put his arm around my shoulders.

"Thank you for standing up for me," he said. "They're good people, Mei-Mei and Drego. They don't have to be right all the time. They're entitled to lose their tempers, to be assholes once in a while. But they're good people. They mean well. Sometimes good intentions don't lead to Hell."

I was embarrassed. Then Michael kissed me lightly on the cheek. I turned to him and he smiled. I couldn't read him.

"What are you thinking?" I asked. Awkward. I probably didn't want to know.

"I think, for the moment, you were thinking about me, not about the movement, or the conference, or anything else," he said. "My heart is jumping around looking for a place to land."

I'm available, I think.

"I'll apologize to Mei-Mei," I said.

"Not just yet," Michael said. "Give her time to deal with her anger. We'll all get back together again. Don't worry."

"Then you're not pissed at me?"

"Dahlia, sometimes when you're onstage and what you're playing just sounds like noise and nobody seems to do what's right, you know the level of talent you've got behind you and you give it a chance to happen," Michael says. "Sometimes it doesn't happen, but when it does . . . when it does, it can be the most beautiful sound in the world. We've got the talent here. Let's let it happen."

I thought I was going to fall as I walked away from him. But I didn't.

He didn't know who I really was.

My biography:

Dahlia Grillo. Father is—was—Juan Grillo, accountant in the Dominican Republic, cabdriver in the Bronx. His famous quote: "Life goes on with or without you." Mother is—was—Estrella García Colón. Waitress in the South

Bronx, left for the West Bronx to move up in the world. Her famous quote: "Know what's in your head, not just what's in your heart." Died of pneumonia waiting for a new Medicaid card.

I got into numbers in elementary school and liked them a lot more than I liked people. Or maybe I just trusted them more. I didn't have a famous quote.

Sometimes I wanted to be a housewife pushing a stroller through the park. Other times I wanted to be just mindlessly happy. What was wrong with that?

I was *seriously* thinking of adopting Anja. She was so together. It was still early and Michael wanted to discuss
whether we should meet with Sayeed's group. Anja said
we should go to Stonehenge and we could talk about it on
the journey there. It would take us away from the hotel
and give us a chance to see something other than each
other. Way cool, Anja.

The weather was cold and rainy and gray. We were
traveling in a rented van and Tristan was driving. Drego
was teasing Tristan, saying he was just faking driving and
he really had the van on automatic, and Tristan almost
smiled. He didn't quite make it, but it was a good effort.

I knew Drego was keeping me and Mei-Mei apart. I felt
bad for blowing her up.

"I assume that most of you looked up Sayeed on the Internet," Michael said. "He acts like some kind of monster. When Morocco gave up its monarchy, he led a group of rebels and took over the area in the High Atlas Mountains. Now he holds the little Moroccan security force at bay and makes raids on whatever group he wants."

"Morocco is largely dependent on tourism, and Sayeed threatens the tourist trade with hotel bombings," Javier added. "All in the name of some mysterious religious sect. God gets blamed again."

"So he's a bad guy," Drego said. "What's he doing in England now? And are you just taking what the Brits are handing out? That their intelligence wants them to stay away from Sayeed?"

"Yeah, that smells right," Anja said. "The English parliament still has one foot in the nineteenth century. They don't want to be near anything that's going to be on the front pages of the tabloids."

"I can see where we might be able to get some useful information from a meeting with this guy," Michael said. "But with them throwing in the bit about British intelligence so late in the game—I'm not sure."

"You think American intelligence isn't onto him?" Javier's voice softened when he spoke to Michael.

"The question is, does our intelligence, or British intelligence, work for the country or for the fat cats who own the country?" Michael said.

"Maybe they just want to meet a rock star." Mei-Mei's voice was shaky. I hoped she was catching a cold.

"People like Sayeed think they're the only stars in the universe," Michael said. "They'll pay any amount of money to get you to perform for them in private, just so they can say they own you."

"You ever perform for somebody in private like that?" Drego asked.

"Yeah, I guess." Michael glanced my way and out the window.

My way? Yes! You worried about what I'm thinking, baby? Are you?

"What can we get from Sayeed that's not already on the Internet?" Drego asked. "There's like a ton of information on him."

"That's the problem." Tristan hunched over the steering wheel as we rounded a turn. "Too much information floating around; you can't follow it all. This guy comes out of every armed conflict he gets into with flying colors. He's not stupid enough to give out information about what he's going to be doing. That doesn't sound like him."

"He works at being a mystery," Javier added.

"Then the feeling is we shouldn't meet with him?" Michael asked.

"If he works at being a mystery," I said, "if he does anything to keep that going, then he's going to leave a footprint. It's like measuring a pyramid. If you can't get to the top of the pyramid, you can still measure its shadow."

"And he's going to hold still for you to measure his shadow?" Javier.

"If we can get a rough count of how many people he has,

we can pretty much scope out the size of his operation," Tristan said. "That's one thing we can figure on."

"And if we get any hints as to where he's going to be operating, maybe we can measure his shadow while he's still moving," Drego said.

It was guy stuff, but it sounded good.

It took an hour and a half to get from London to Stonehenge. Anja started talking about the controversy of the renovations that had taken three years to complete.

"Historians were saying there was more new stuff than old." Anja had a way of talking that made her mouth look as if she was smiling all the time. "The renovations people said that in a few years, all you would have left would be a pile of dust and a few pictures."

We had to climb a small hill to see the stones laid out in a circle. They were big and heavy-looking, and it was hard to imagine moving the stones in a world without wheels and modern machines.

"Dahlia, could you have done a model of the people who built Stonehenge?" Michael asked.

"No." Simple answer. "Too many guesses involved. You don't know the engineering skills of the people who built this place, or their working conditions. Basically, you need to know what was done, and why it was done, and how it was carried out. You can add some theories about what they might do in the future, but you need to start with a base of facts."

"We got enough facts on Sayeed?" Tristan.

"Sayeed's strength is violence," Javier said. His motorized

wheelchair looked like a throne. There was a screen on the left armrest that viewed the area behind the chair. "Can we stop him if there's violence involved?"

"Sayeed is not playing the endgame," Mei-Mei said. "C-8 is playing the endgame and Sayeed is just a strategy."

That made sense.

Stonehenge was disappointing. It did look old, but you knew they had covered the original stones with a plastic material to preserve the original shapes. I think if it had been a dry day, it would have been cool, but the rain on the plastic made the whole scene too shiny. It was like the backdrop for an animated flick. Still, we walked around it for a good half hour, with me thinking that my narrow butt was freezing. Then the rain picked up and we bought a few souvenirs from a vendor at the bottom of the hill and piled back into the van.

"This brochure says that the Stonehenge stones were laid out in a hexagon that faced a particular pattern of stars," Drego said. "A gold plate with a near-identical design belonged to the king of Stonehenge and was popularly known as Britain's first crown jewels. You think there were aliens building this stuff?"

"Dahlia doesn't think so." Anja.

How did she know that?

"Dahlia?" Javier.

"Almost everything has some kind of structure. Read Plato. You have structures and patterns that repeat themselves in nature," I said. "Some we've seen all our lives and just kind of recognize, or maybe we just recognize the ones we like. But the easiest thing in the world is to make too much of them. You can go crazy digging up explanations of stuff you don't understand."

"So some shit is just mysterious?" Tristan said.

"Something like that," I answered.

"Dahlia, you think Sayeed is just mysterious?"

"We know more or less who he is," I said. "Like Tristan and Drego were saying, if we add in other pieces of information, we can plot him out. If the stuff he's done in the past is more or less consistent with what he's done recently, we can make pretty good predictions."

"Drego?" Michael pointed toward where Drego and Mei-Mei sat together.

"Can't tell right now," Drego said. "Like Tristan said, if we know how many people he's got, we can figure the size of his move. If we know where he's planning a move, we'll know even more. The best thing to do might be just to beat the crap out of the Brits to make sure they're giving us everything they got and not just using us."

"Javier?"

"I can optimize our resources, get things moving," Javier said. "It's really iffy if you have to pick up the information as you go along."

"Mei-Mei?"

Her face twisted and then hardened. She cut her eyes toward me and exhaled heavily. She had dissed Michael, and now he was asking her opinion. I could feel her thinking about what she should do.

She exhaled.

"I know the difference between just making moves, or

just doing computer models, and a real endgame," Mei-Mei said. "All the computer models in the world won't get you a bowl of soup if they're not right and on time. I don't see Sayeed passing out any terrorist manuals."

"Anja?"

"If he meets with us, he won't be able to resist trying to impress us." Anja rested her chin on her fist. "And every time he opens his mouth, he'll give something up if we read it right."

Mei-Mei was staring daggers at Anja. I could see how she would be a good chess player. She had a killer instinct, and she turned it against anybody and everybody.

"Tristan?"

"I do what I do," Tristan said. "And I do it good."

It wasn't the right answer, or even a clear answer, but people didn't mess with Tristan.

"You sure?" Drego asked.

"I'm sure I can bring whatever fight we need to engage in together," Tristan said. "What you guys decide you want to do with Sayeed, I'll make happen."

We rode the next forty-five minutes in silence. Getting into London was brutal. The Underground was shut down and buses were being rerouted away from the Central Zone, which meant that to get anywhere, you had to circle the outskirts of the city and wait until some traffic officer let you down a path you hoped would lead you to where you wanted to go. Everything was rerouted around Hyde Park, and we were all getting hungry and I had to go to the bathroom.

"Do we want to vote on meeting Sayeed?" Michael

asked. We were sitting in traffic in Bayswater. There were a lot of small hotels along the way, and people bent like question marks under black umbrellas moving through the mist.

At first nobody answered; then Drego said that he voted yes.

One by one we all voted yes.

Why? I thought the guys were eager to fight, especially Drego and Tristan. Michael was doing what he thought was right, and I wasn't 100 percent sure what that meant. I didn't know anything about Javier. Mei-Mei—I expected her to go along with Drego.

Anja. I didn't think of her as a fighter, but I didn't think of her as someone who would back down either. She was good people. Period.

Me, I voted yes and then asked myself if I had voted just to support Michael.

I thought he was pulling it off. Pulling the band together, getting all the right people into all the right places and giving us freedom to do our own thing. He was definitely working it.

What I didn't know was why the hell Sayeed wanted to meet with us. Why were we so important to everybody?

11

"Are you still feeling good about meeting with this Sayeed character?" I was pouring two capfuls of something called Persil into the washing machine.

"He's a big-time creep," Anja said. She was popping seedless grapes into her mouth at record speed. "But I want to do something. You know, storm the barricades or march through Valley Forge. Maybe we're all in that boat. We watch good people do nothing—didn't somebody say something about that? Some poet talking about good people doing nothing while the bad guys jig around?"

"Could be," I said. "I've never been into poetry. You try this washing machine yet?"

Each of our apartments had a small washing machine

that looked like it was a hundred years old. Somebody had dropped the instructions on how to use it in water, so I was playing it by ear.

"I washed some things by hand," Anja said. "The guys and Mei-Mei sent their stuff out."

"They told you that?"

"Mei-Mei told me," Anja said.

"She didn't tell me," I said.

"That's because she's competing with you," Anja said, pushing the grapes away. "She needs to cover up that nagging feeling she has that she's only as good as her last review, or her last chess ranking. She doesn't see me as much competition. Don't let her bother you."

"I just don't want to be the one who screws up," I said.

"Good."

"Good?"

"Yeah—we're beginning to feel like a team, right?"

"Now I *really* don't want to screw up," I said. "And don't say 'good' again."

"You won't screw up," Anja said. "We're feeling our way in the dark. Everybody knows that. But you don't have a mean streak. Sometimes I think it's good to have a mean streak—it lets you cover up your doubts."

"That's deep."

"I read it someplace," Anja said. "Usually, if I read something good, I remember it. But I never remember where I read it. If I could do that, I'd be like—I don't know—smart sounding or something."

"You're smart enough," I said. "Michael wouldn't have you here if you weren't."

"More team stuff, Dahlia." Anja smiled and reached for the grapes again. "You're going to be okay."

"I don't know. I started a model based on all the news items I found about Sayeed. With all the crap he's done—shooting up villages, taking food supplies—how come he was under the radar for so long?"

"Maybe because he was just one more foul thing happening in a sea of bad things," Anja said. "You can't keep up with everything. Did you find anything interesting?"

"No."

"That's okay," she said. "You'll get it together."

The washing machine started shaking like it was going to take off through the ceiling, and we both went over and looked at it. I thought about pulling out the plug, then changed my mind. We watched it for another twenty seconds, and then it stopped shaking and started humming.

"E-flat," Anja said. "It's got soul!"

"Take the grapes," I said as Anja was leaving. She had made me feel good about myself when I'd hoped I wasn't letting my mouth lead me to places I couldn't really get to.

It was all settled. We were going to meet with Sayeed. Michael was giving us details about what Victor wanted to know about Sayeed's strength. Drego and Tristan were listening to every word, but Mei-Mei looked distant. I knew she was recording the conversation in her little brain, taking it down syllable by syllable. Later, she'd play it back for Drego and criticize Michael. I was already nervous, as much for Michael as for myself. He didn't look as confident as Drego, or Tristan, or even Mei-Mei.

Edgeware Road. There were rows of shops with Arabic signs, and restaurants with dark guys and light-skinned girls at tables in front of them smoking hookahs. I didn't think all the girls were Middle Eastern, but it was hard to tell. London wasn't nearly as white as I'd thought it would be. We went to a narrow building next to what looked like a club of some sort. Victor had asked if one of his people could "tag along," but Michael had said no.

"Their working with British intelligence makes me jumpy," he said.

The way Javier talked, I felt that the group Michael had put together hadn't been formed very long ago. I also wondered if Michael really knew Mei-Mei and Drego anymore. They were very much a team. She hung out with him all the time, making sure that some part of her body was touching his. I wondered how they touched when they were alone.

Crap! There was no access for Javier's chair! Drego and Tristan offered to carry him up the stairs, but he was dead set against it.

"I'll wait in the van," he said.

It was a sad moment. The team was being split up by something as stupid as wheelchair access. I was immediately pissed at England. Nobody wanted to make a big deal of it, but it was a big deal for all of us.

Up a narrow flight of stairs. The room we entered was illuminated by yellowish lanterns set into the ceiling. There was a red couch against one wall. Against another was a table with what looked like a damask tablecloth. It caught the light from the ceiling and from the candles placed at either end. There were chairs around the table, high backed and tufted. It was all very dramatic. Drama is always about trying to put something fake on the table, and I relaxed when I saw it. The adjoining room was set off from us by four stained-glass panels. A delicate balance of colors showed an orange tree surrounded by peacocks.

In my head, I went over the dossier the Brits had supplied about Sayeed. He had emerged from a village in the High Atlas Mountains some three years earlier. He was between the ages of seventeen and twenty and had put together a force of some eight hundred to twelve hundred young fighters. He had no known family. To some Moroccans he was heroic, but to the Brits he was just a terrorist being raised on the pedestal of his crimes.

The room was empty except for the sounds of the rhythmic music drifting up from the floor below. A fan turned lazily in a corner, barely moving the heavy air.

For a moment we all stood awkwardly, waiting while our eyes grew accustomed to the low light. Then we positioned ourselves on one side of the table, our backs toward the door. In my paranoia, I channeled an old cowboy movie I once saw where a sheriff said to always sit with your back to a wall.

Tristan was sitting at one end of the table and Drego near the middle. Mei-Mei was next to Drego, and Michael was still standing. Anja and I were sitting at the other end.

Minutes went by. Sayeed was late. More drama, or maybe he wasn't coming. Then there was a shuffling on the stairway, and I turned as Sayeed's crew entered the room. There were only four people. They came in, took a moment to see how we were situated, and took seats across from us.

One of their people was a heavy-shouldered guy who looked as if he could have been an American football player. Muscle.

The second was a very nervous-looking kid who was drumming his fingers almost before he was fully seated. Nervous Guy was yellowish brown. Brains.

The third was brown-skinned with round cheeks and heavy glasses. He looked out of place.

Then there was Sayeed. He was very tall and stood for a moment to show off his height. He was dressed in a white, loose-fitting robe with the headdress of an Arab chieftain. His broad forehead and dark eyes topped a classic bone structure that tapered down into a neat goatee. It was Black Jesus time.

"So, you have arranged a meeting with Sayeed," he said. His voice was deep, resonant. The accent was slight but there. "What information are you digging for, my American friends?"

"We thought that people with common interests should get to know each other," Michael said as he sat down.

"The entertainer!" Sayeed gestured at Michael as he spoke to his guys. Then, slowly, he turned toward him. "Do you want to exchange dance moves?"

The challenge.

Michael put his hand to his chin and shrugged. "We don't have a lot of time to waste," he said. "If you're not interested . . ."

"Don't be impatient," Sayeed said. Then to his own guys, as if he was interpreting us, "That's an American habit—impatience."

Michael leaned back in his chair. We heard more steps on the stairs, and I imagined they were more of Sayeed's crew. I was relieved to see three young boys bringing bowls of fruit and small cakes. No one spoke as they placed them on the table before us, then quickly left.

"What shall I call you?" Sayeed looked at Michael. "When you performed with your band—was it called The Cave?"

"Plato's Cave," Michael said.

"Yes, an interesting name for a Western group," Sayeed went on. "The illusion of reality and all that. And you, of course, are Michael."

"That's good enough," Michael said.

"Michael, we might have common interests, but I don't know what they are," Sayeed continued. "I came to England to see what this 'convention' was about. All my people tell me is that it was about beautiful people making pretty speeches. I missed the entire point of it."

"No, you didn't miss the point," Michael responded. "You read the papers that came out of the conference and the papers leading up to it. You know what it was about. Why didn't you join us? You're young; you have an interest in the world and what we can make of it."

"Is that what you're about? Saving the world?" Sayeed turned to Muscle Guy. "Haven't we heard about how Americans save the world?"

Muscle Guy chuckled to himself. Maybe itself.

"Sayeed—may I call you Sayeed?" Michael pushed a bit of pastry around with his finger as he talked. I felt he was growing more confident.

"Please."

"Sayeed, we can sit here and posture all evening if that's what you want to do," Michael said. "Or we can come to a clearer understanding of our positions. The more we know about each other, the more likely we are to avoid conflicts."

"Maged, explain to the Americans who we are!" Sayeed spoke without looking at any of his people.

Nervous Guy glanced at Sayeed, sniffed twice, and then took a pad from his jacket.

"We are an army of twelve thousand fighters," he said. He paused to let his statement sink in. "Each of our warriors has an automatic weapon and a backup firearm. We have rocket-propelled grenades, artillery, drones, vehicles, and sufficient energy reserves to fight for seven years and six months. We do not expect anyone in the world to be able to stand against us unless they have a potent air force, such as the one we are developing."

"Impressive numbers," Michael said. "And something of a surprise."

Sayeed laughed. It was a higher laugh than I'd thought he would have. Black Jesus cracking up over a joke on the hills overlooking Jerusalem. "What I like about Americans is your arrogance!" he said. "You believe only what you want to believe, and then you force the world to think what you think. Or do you think that I will now offer proofs to you? Give you my sources? Perhaps send you a copy of my diary? Is that what you want?"

There was a hint of anger in his voice.

Next to me, Anja laid her pencil down, the point facing

away from me. She was using the code we had agreed on, saying that Sayeed was lying, but about what?

"We don't have your numbers, Sayeed," Michael said. "Or your weapons. But we could get them—anyone could get them in today's world—so why should we be impressed?"

"When you can change the hearts that beat within the peoples of North Africa," Sayeed said, "I will be impressed. When you can change our history and the degradation we have suffered over the last seven decades, I will be impressed. When you wipe away the cheapness of our lives, then, and only then, will I bow to you!"

Anja turned the pencil. Sayeed was speaking from his heart.

Silence. Sayeed had taken the floor, and he commanded the room. Tristan was eating grapes. Drego stared down at his hands.

An idea. "Did you fly to England from Casablanca?" I asked.

"You are comic relief?" Sayeed looked at me. His lips flattened and turned into a sneer. He'd lost the moment.

"A simple question," I answered. "It came to mind. I didn't know it would be a secret."

"We were flown directly from Menara Airport in Marrakech," he answered. "A small fleet of private planes. Have you ever been to Menara Airport?"

"I've seen pictures of it," I said. "Quite beautiful."

"Michael, you should send your women as my guests," Sayeed said. "They can learn something about a different culture."

"I didn't know commercial airlines were still flying out of Menara," I went on, ignoring Sayeed's sexist invitation. "Since the terrorist attacks a few years ago."

"Terrorist attacks." Sayeed looked away and then back toward the fruit in front of him. Carefully, he picked up a banana and slowly stripped away the peel. "What Americans love to do is to take away those layers of protection each man has until they reach the core, his basic humanity. Then they label it terrorist and destroy it."

He bit into the banana.

"Well, I'm glad to hear that they've resumed flights into that airport," I said. "If the women did want to come to learn something about 'a different culture,' how would we reach you?"

"You've managed to reach me tonight," Sayeed answered. "Reach me again and I'll arrange your flights."

"Why did you only bring three of your staff to this meeting?" I asked.

"If I had known you would be here," Sayeed said, "I would have brought more to see your great beauty. But you will come to my humble mountains, flown into Menara on planes that start from your Newark Airport, and I will show you the same army that took Spain in the eighth century. I give you my word on this."

"The trouble with words, Sayeed," Michael said as he twisted in his chair, "is that they are so cheap that almost everyone has too many of them."

Sayeed was on his feet immediately. "I could slit your throats this evening and no one would ever hear of you again!" he said. "You would be just another useless rumor that even your kind would soon forget. *Whatever* your kind is!"

Michael might have pushed Sayeed too much. We had walked into this restaurant unarmed. Most of the men in the restaurant were dark-skinned, perhaps even Sayeed's men. I looked at Michael. He didn't seem as nervous as I felt.

"Sayeed, I received a fancy pouch and a letter that said that you wanted to meet with *les Américains* without telling us what you want. Now we are here. Are you embarrassed?"

"Women are embarrassed, Michael, not warriors," Sayeed said. "I wanted to see for myself the illusion you flash on the wall. No, I am not embarrassed. I have seen what I came to see, and dismiss it, and you, from the corners of my mind."

"I guess I'll have to try to forget you, too," Michael said.

"One day, Michael, I will surprise you!" Sayeed sat down. "You will hear your doorbell ring, and when you answer it, I will be standing in front of your home with a smile on my face. Look at me. I know you are thinking that we are just another of your petty *favelos*. We know how you like them—brave little bands of struggling kids that you can dismiss from your mind. Play your songs as they disappear into the sunset. How romantic! We're not like them. We have an army, the weapons, and enough fuel to reach you wherever you hide. *Wherever* you hide. And now, because I hate being bored, I will call this meeting over. Go home, and close your eyes, and enjoy your fantasies."

Sayeed stood and his crew stood with him. More theatrics. They stalked out, trying to look angry. I felt myself relaxing. We hadn't been killed.

I looked over at Mei-Mei. Her brow was shiny with sweat. Interesting. Drego was quiet. I looked at Tristan. Calm. At least on the outside.

Back to the hotel. It was dark and the streets glistened with rain. Javier was at the controls and Michael was describing to him what had happened at the meeting.

"It was very short," Javier said.

"He just wanted to impress us," Michael said. "He knew what he was going to do and say before he ever got there."

"You thinking he's just selling wolf tickets?" Drego.

"Yeah, more or less," Michael said. "In the long run, he's still in North Africa and there's not a lot he can do to be effective against C-8. That's the important thing. And they don't really need him."

"They came out and got into two limousines," Javier said. "The first had Sayeed and three guys, and the second had guys with suspicious-looking bundles. Probably weapons."

"You could tell which one was Sayeed?" Anja asked.

"All he needed was a drum roll," Javier said. "He announced himself pretty well."

Michael asked Anja what she had made of Sayeed.

"I think he was bragging about a lot of things," she said. "But he believed most of what he was saying. The figures might have been off, but it wasn't all lies. At least that's what I got from him. That and a coldness. It was as if he didn't have regular feelings."

Michael said he thought Sayeed was mostly about bravado, and Drego agreed. Tristan just kind of grunted, and Mei-Mei rubbed Drego's arm.

"Dahlia?" I could see just the outline of Michael's face as we passed the London Hilton on Park Lane Hotel.

"I haven't figured out why he came to the meeting yet," I said. "I need to think about it more."

"Did you think Sayeed was seriously thinking about slitting our throats?" I was back at the hotel, talking with Anja on the phone.

"No," I lied.

"You're lying," Anja said. "I thought so too."

In bed, trying to decide if I liked London or not, when the phone rang again. I thought it was Anja calling back, but it was Tristan.

"Where were you going with that stuff about the airport?" he asked. "That was just something to say, or . . . ?"

"I was just trying to get at who was financing Sayeed," I said. "Flying takes money. Or did he drive the distance? It would take about two and a half days to drive, but it would be cheaper. I'd just like to know."

"You didn't say anything to Javier," Tristan said.

"Right," I answered.

"You going to?"

I felt like he was confronting me, and I didn't like it. But I said I would in the morning.

"Maybe tonight?"

"Yeah."

"I think it might be the only thing we came away with," Tristan said. "He was defensive about it."

Tristan hung up.

I had been fishing when I'd asked the question about flying, and I didn't really know what to say to Javier. I called him and told him that Tristan thought I should mention it. Javier said he would check the flights out of Marrakech.

"There's not a lot of traffic from that airport," he said.

13

Going home! I had been away for eighteen years! Or was it less than a week? At the airport. Victor and two cool-looking guys in turtleneck sweaters met us for breakfast. Tristan ran down the meeting with Sayeed and said we didn't believe his numbers or his organization.

"I tend to believe him," Victor said. "And he scares me. He's just ambitious enough to launch an attack anywhere in the world. He starts spouting history, stupid stuff mostly, and places himself squarely in the middle of some great adventure. People like that have a different sense of mortality than we do."

"What do you know about his connections with C-8—are they real?" Michael asked.

"C-8 has real connections with everything in the freaking world," one of Victor's guys said. "I don't think his bragging about him having access to money means anything. In your country, somebody from the Ku Klux Klan can say he had a connection with Martin Luther King because he tried to firebomb him."

"Sayeed's very much like the Sturmers," Victor added. "He doesn't have much going on outside the fame he gets from being a butcher, so he's going to stay with it. The thing that bothers me is he's getting louder, and C-8 is acting out of character, but they are still predicting economic growth."

"You mean that they're going to steal more!" Mei-Mei said.

"Whatever you want to call it," Victor said. "It's puzzling. We'll keep working on it and sharing information with you. I hope we can rely on you to do the same?"

"Yes," Michael said.

On the plane.

"Victor told me that Sayeed was flashing all over the Net about his meeting with us," Michael said. "He didn't have anything good to say about it, but just his flashing it is significant. He thinks he did all right."

"Well, we certainly didn't look good," Mei-Mei jumped in. "They set the place and the time, and they controlled the conversation. We ate grapes and listened."

"I'm thinking we should give ourselves a chance to analyze it," Michael said.

"That's French for 'make stuff up.'" Drego. He and Mei-Mei were getting to be an act.

We were in a cabin that used to be called first class, when it held two people rich enough to afford it. Now it was called cram section, because we were all crammed into it.

"The Brits set up the meeting to assess what was going on in the world," Michael said. "They have the best intelligence—"

"—which they aren't sharing with anyone," Drego reminded us.

"Which they aren't particularly sharing with us," Michael said. "But so far, it's been the best. If all Sayeed has to celebrate is how he talked to the Americans, then we did all right."

"Michael, let me ask you this." Drego wet his lips. "How do you know that Victor isn't making alliances? How do you know he isn't looking ahead and getting his people ready to team up with a group of fighters? Like Sayeed."

"I don't know it," Michael said. "But if I can't know everything that's going on, I'd better be damned sure I know who my friends are."

Drego and Mei-Mei shut down. I had wanted to talk over my models, but I didn't want to do it if Drego and Mei-Mei were shaky. And they were shaky.

Anja was reading British newspapers and business magazines. When she got up to get snacks, she asked me if I wanted anything. I went with her to the tiny kitchen between the cabins. They had freshly baked cookies and little paper cups of some kind of delicious custard.

"I think Javier wants to talk to you," Anja said.

"About what?" I asked.

"I don't know, but he keeps looking over in your direction."

I decided that Anja was some kind of psychic. Really weird, but I liked her being on my side.

When we got back, Mei-Mei saw what we had gotten to eat and, predictably, went and got food for her and Drego. Michael had fallen asleep, and I went over and sat next to Javier.

"How's it going?" I asked.

"Okay," he said. "I checked the airport—Menara—and found that Natural Farming booked flights to London around the same time Sayeed came. It can't be a coincidence that a C-8 corporation left Menara the same time Sayeed did. I figured they must have booked the flights for him."

"That's deep," I said, "but I don't know where to go from here. What the hell are they up to?"

"I bet there's going to be some stink to it," Javier said.

"Ya think?" I said.

"Yeah, it was a good pickup," Javier said.

He didn't seem excited about it or anything, and I didn't know if I should run to Michael with it or not. The thing was that Mei-Mei and Drego seemed to be going their own way, and I didn't know if they were even going to stay with the group. I knew Michael wanted to give everybody a chance to do their thing, but I was getting a real bad feeling about it all. What the hell was I missing?

I knew it wasn't real, but I thought I smelled some of

Mrs. Rosario's stew. Maybe some time at home would clear my head.

We landed at Newark, breezed through customs, and started saying good-byes. I wanted Michael to do or say something that was cheerleading or at least comforting, but he didn't.

Tristan's dad, a veteran who had lost his legs in some war a million years ago, was there to meet him.

"We'll regroup at my place as soon as possible," Michael said. "If everybody made reports about what they felt went down in London, it would be useful. We need to fill in as many gaps as we can."

Anja, Drego, and Mei-Mei started walking toward the taxi stand. I followed them.

Clearly, Michael needed some space. Mei-Mei and Drego had shaken his confidence big-time. Or maybe the tension had just gotten to us all. We had gone to the conference because C-8 was kicking our collective ass. It was still kicking ass and making new plans, and we were still in the dark.

Over the next few days the underground blogs carried their versions of what had gone down at the conference. Stupid headlines, like "Dodging the Doldrums in Dullwich," ran over super-serious pictures of the delegates looking glum. Most of the papers carried the same message: that nothing had been accomplished, and that our message wasn't clear. There was at least one reference in each story to the Occupy movement of twenty years earlier.

In the Bronx.

On a whim, or the breeze stirred up by a whiff of nerve, I texted the Brit kid who did their computer work and asked him to send me any computer models he had done as a result of the conference. "And I will send you mine, of course."

His text reply was shorter than my message. It read, simply, "No."

I ran my models again and again, looking for anything I could report. The 2-percent "growth" meant that C-8 was on the move, and the world was holding its breath to find out what that move was.

Me lying on the bed, understanding crawling through my body like the flu. I was hot and sweaty and a little sick, but I was beginning to understand more than I ever had before. We had traveled all the way to England, had talked our asses off, and nothing had changed. Drego and Mei-Mei weren't just creeps—they had to feel the same way I did. Discouraged. Hopeless. Shitty. What I had been see-ing all around me for years were people who had just given up, who had just "stopped singing." Now, maybe, it was my turn to shut up and close my eyes.

I thought about Morristown, about how my friends could visit me if I lived there. You just didn't get on a bus anymore. You figured who was headed in your general di-rection, how much you could trust them, and how little information you could pass along. Morristown was sur-rounded by Gater communities, so once you got within five miles, you were relatively safe from roving *favelo* squads. There was a lot of old, smart money in towns like Madison and Maplewood, and they had built their fortresses early. I wasn't going to let a little risk keep me from the meeting.

Back to the computer. Assembling and disassembling the models. Making small adjustments, forcing myself to answer the same questions again and again.

What did I know? That C-8 never did anything that wasn't in their interest. Now they were acting as if they wanted to change a little, but still boasting about a 2-percent increase in growth. We knew most of C-8's actions and we sensed—really, we knew—that they hadn't changed. We saw the similarities, *but where were the differences?*

I looked at the models I had constructed about the Nigerian oil business. The Brits had controlled Nigerian oil at one time, and there was plenty of data on income and barrels produced. Once C-8 had taken over control, the income remained steady and the expenditures went down. The fuckers were efficient. The question was, why were they giving up a percentage of their projected revenue to the Nigerians? My old Epson printer had spit out pages of multicolored graphs that looked enough alike to make you go blind. I typed in the question again. *Where was the difference?*

The other part of the equation was a C-8 company's connection to Sayeed. It wasn't like them to connect to anything negative, and I couldn't find anything in the news files that made Sayeed look even vaguely positive.

Anxiety dream. Me and Mei-Mei have an argument and I get into her face. She's good with words, spits her rap like she's been practicing, but I get to her by grabbing her by her throat and pushing her against the wall. Pure ghetto. Then Drego punches me in the face and I wake up. Lousy dream. Close my eyes. Wake up. Close my eyes. Wake up. Check the clock. It was only twelve-thirty, which meant I probably wouldn't get a bunch of sleep all night.

Switched my night dream to a daydream. Me punching out Mei-Mei and then punching out Drego. It wasn't going to happen, but I liked the daydream better. I reminded myself that Mei-Mei and Drego were not the enemy. They just didn't deal with their frustrations well.

In the morning, Mrs. Rosario knocked on my door and asked if I wanted to have some *aguaji*. It was just what I needed.

"You look more skinny!" she said. "How was England?"

"Interesting," I answered. "I think they're more comfortable with their lives than we are."

"They don't have little towns with gates around them like we do?" she asked.

"They have them, but it's like okay with them or something," I said. "The English are a bit cold, I think."

"Take the soup."

The sliced plantains were pale in the clear broth, and the tiny flakes of cilantro and chilies were inviting. And sooo warm going in.

Rafael showed up wearing his wifebeater undershirt, walking in without knocking as per usual, and sat down next to me.

"Mrs. Rosario and I were looking in books about England

when you were gone. I saw some places I wanted to see when I was young. You know, I was almost in England once," he said. "When I was twenty—maybe twenty-two. I almost went."

I liked the idea that Mrs. Rosario had been following my trip. I liked being home again too.

"If any of us ever gets rich, we should all go to England for a few weeks." Something to say.

"I'll never get rich," Rafael said. "It's not good for you. You get rich and you lose your insides, the stuff that makes you real."

Mrs. Rosario got on Rafael's case about him not being ambitious enough to get rich, and he defended his status as a poor man. It was the wisdom of the DR and, along with the *aguaji*, comforting.

14

Lying on the bed. It was narrower than I remembered, and firmer. Why is it harder to remember things I am so familiar with? Weird. I was more tired than I should be, I thought. Everything was suddenly a choice. Did I want to change into a nightgown or lie here in my jeans and T-shirt? What I wanted was a simple life. Eat. Sleep. Work. Look for hope. In a C-8 world it was even simpler. See what they have given you to eat. See where they let you sleep. Wonder what there is to hope for. My phone buzzed. I picked it up and saw there was a text message from Anja.

A: Dahlia, I am sooo hungry but tooo lazy to even cut up a melon. How are you doing?

D: Not bad. Feel a little like I've been running on a treadmill for fifty years

A: #Got that# When I first met up with Michael, I thought it was all going to be fast track to glory, or whatever.

D: How did you run into him?

A: At a fair trade conference. Everybody was talking about getting a good deal for the small farmers in Colombia. Idealistic stuff. You know it. After the meetings, people broke up and had drinks (maybe fair trade cocktails for the small bartenders in Pittsburgh—LOL). Anyway, the whites were sitting with the whites and the mightys were sitting with the mightys, and I was talking to some of the women who worked the farms. That's where M found me. I kind of blend in with people, I guess, and he liked that.

D: You blend in big-time, but that's like your gift, right? There are people I couldn't blend in with. Like M-M. Or Drego.

A: D—You blend in if there's a math path.

D: Some people don't have math parts, or maybe they just don't recognize them. What are you thinking about eating?

A: I have a cantaloupe in the fridge. Then there's some containers of Greek yogurt that might not have gone bad. Problem: if I eat something, maybe my brain will start working again. Now, do I want my brain working again or do I just want to veg out?

D: We're running out of things to think about anyway. I got nothing out of the Dulwich set—a lot less from the friggin' Sturmers, and zilch plus minus zilch from Sayeed. There was such a sneer on his face, it looked like he was going into convulsions.

A: He's good-looking, though.

D: No way!

A: D—I think we got something out of those meetings. I was thinking—it happens every now and then—and wondering why M asked me to join the group. I think he picked a crew with different abilities. Like he picked a band. Know what I mean?

D: What did he pick M-M for? She's a bitch!

A: You get the feeling that inside that little head all kinds of gears are turning?

D: No. Just stink bombs going off.

A: What I came away with was somebody saying—was it you?—that we needed to figure out why everybody is interested in us.

D: Because we're cute?

A: Well, that's the main reason, but why else? Just because we're Americans?

D: You think C-8 is thinking about letting something big jump off in the States?

A: They wouldn't dare. There's not that much testosterone in the world.

D: You said they were true believers. They don't have to have the balls if they believe hard enough. Anyway, I wouldn't put it past them.

A: The thing is that they can find some little scraps of "right" in their arguments—you know, progress or something like that—and they take that and run with it as if it's the Holy Grail.

D: I don't know. Hey, got another text message coming in. From Javier. I'll ghost it to your phone.

A: You going to tell him I'm listening in?

D: No. No way it's personal from Javier.

J: Dahlia. Javier here. I got a message from an old friend. We used to be pretty close. She's a technician, and the stuff she's saying is pretty complex. Michael thinks you might be able to understand it.

A: Michael got Javier to text? Dahlia—isn't that strange?

D: Javier. Good to hear from you. I'm okay with most science stuff. What is your friend saying?

J: She's depressed over what she calls some pretty serious shit. But she was always a little weepy. If you don't want to deal with it, we can let it drop. She called in the early AM. I don't know if her line was secure or not.

D: I can deal with it.

A: D—ask him who she's a technician for.

D: Javier, who does she work for?

J: CTI, C-8's medical arm. She's a lab techie.

A: Dahlia, we're onto something!

J: She might be losing it. I don't know. Michael thinks ... I don't know....

D: You want me to call her?

J: It might be better. We need to figure out a way to establish contact without compromising her.

D: Especially if she's your friend.

J: That's not the issue, Dahlia.

D: Okay. Okay.

A: D—ask him if she's willing to talk to you.

D: She probably just needs to talk to somebody, Javier. You get me the details and I'll check her out. No problem.

J: I'll clear it with Michael—see what he wants to do. Talk to you later.

D: Okay.

D: Anja, he's off the circuit. What did you make of that? Wait, I'm getting another text. It's from Michael.

M: Dahlia, this is Michael—something has come up. Javier will call or text you—probably within the next hour or so. There's somebody in Minnesota who we might want to contact. I don't know a lot about it yet, but I know Javier's a little nuts. It sounds like an old girlfriend or something. Don't get mad if it starts to get frustrating. I've never seen Javier this upset before.

D: Yeah. Okay. Michael, I just talked to Javier. I think he needs me to talk to this girl. Doesn't sound like a big deal, but I'll get on it.

M: Good. I don't know how big a deal it is either. But what I do know is that we have a direct link to a C-8 company, so we have to see if there's a change in the rhythm. Maybe you can analyze how it connects together. I think we need to get people focused on different groups. Maybe you can home in on Javier's contact in Minnesota.

D: Michael, it's Javier's contact. Why doesn't he deal with it?

M: He's close to weirding out on me now. I can't afford to lose him. We can't afford to lose him. I'm having him and Mei-Mei keep an eye on Sayeed's group.

D: Why Mei-Mei?

M: She speaks Arabic. Dahlia, you're the one for this. Later.

D: Anja, Michael's off. What's going on?

A: If Javier is upset, there must be a reason. If Michael is reaching out to you, there must be a reason too. And this technician works for a C-8 company, right?

D: Yeah?

A: So ... yeah. But is there something they're not telling us?

D: Javier said that M told him to run it by me. And he ran it by me even before M thought he would. Were you ever suspicious that Michael was holding back on us?

A: Not really. The group is so diverse. What did Lincoln say—you can't fool anybody—something like that?

D: Then it's Javier who knows more than his prayers.

A: What does that mean?

D: It means that we're getting pieces of a puzzle to put together, and we don't know what the finished picture looks like. But if we get enough pieces, we'll be able to figure it out.

A: Oh, that sounds so smart. Give yourself a pat on the back. Especially that bit about Michael wanting to reach out through you. He must think the modeling is working.

D: I didn't say that.

A: You were probably going to.

D: I need to go find some more to eat.

A: Dahlia, don't underestimate yourself on this.

D: Can you imagine M-M speaking Arabic? That really pisses me off.

A: Can you imagine how pissed you'd be if you were edgy? My, my! Later, Dahlia darling.

As I shut off the cell, I remembered a box of crackers I had in my closet. I found them. They were stale, but mucho delicious.

15

"Dahlia, you are *not* being dissed!" Anja said.

"Then why are we on the plane coming into St. Paul to have a talk with a girl who Javier could have had on the phone?" I said. "Meanwhile Mei-Mei is busy tracking down Sayeed in North Africa!"

"And you're mad because she speaks Arabic!"

"I just don't get the picture," I said.

"There's something more to Javier's embarrassment when he talks about this girl," Anja said. "I don't get it either, but I guess we'll find out. I hope you're never mad at me!"

I mumbled something about being sorry and told myself to get my mind back to work. Anja was on the money when she said that I was letting Mei-Mei get on my nerves.

On the ground, in a taxi, and checking in at the Crowne Plaza, St. Paul, Minnesota. The guards in the lobby were all white. Big, beefy guys who might have played football. Anja's FoneTrac 8 was really too big to carry around, but she had it with her anyway. I watched over her shoulder as she scrolled through an animated history of the city. She read to me that Minnesota had the largest white urban community in the United States.

"I thought the clerk was giving me funny looks when we checked in," I said when we got to the room.

"You're a little brown-skinned girl checking into a luxury hotel," Anja said. "And you have a car in their lot waiting for you, so you must be somebody. I think he was expecting you to announce your title or something."

I caught a glimpse of myself in the hotel mirror. Not bad, but I needed a comb.

"You want to get something to eat?" Anja asked. "You drive, I'll eat."

"I don't drive," I said. "You didn't say anything when Michael said he would arrange for a car to be at the hotel for us, so I thought you drove."

"You didn't say anything, so I thought *you* drove!"

We were laughing and it felt really good.

"You think it's one of those cars that drive themselves?" I asked.

Anja checked the itinerary that Michael had given us and found that the car was an automatic with GPS guidance.

The café at which we were supposed to meet Ellen Chai-kin, Javier's contact, was only two miles from the hotel, but we decided to cab it.

"You're going to the Pig's Eye Café in Rondoville?" The cabdriver squinted through his clear left lens. "That's where you're going?"

"Yeah." Anja. "You know where it is?"

"Get in."

Four over-the-speed-limit minutes later, we arrived at a barbed-wire gate with armed guards. They were either Sturmers or Sturmer wannabes. A short, roundish dude with a baby face looked at the driver and then back at me and Anja.

"More working girls?"

"Could be." The cabdriver.

They rolled aside the barbed-wire gate and let us through. Anja asked for the driver's number. He said he didn't give it out. Abrupt. To the point.

"There's a long way here," he said. "Around the lake road and through the new development. It'll cost you twice as much and you'll have to pay both ways for a cab to pick you up. If one will come out here. Twelve minutes at the most."

It was what the world had come to, gates and "safe routes" and cars sliding through the night. It was what C-8 had built and was trying to keep going. And Michael and me and Anja and our little crew were trying hard to be more than road bumps in their path.

Inside the Pig's Eye Café. The gaudy decor wasn't as bad

as the stupid music, and the stupid music wasn't as bad as the stickiness of the floor. We found a booth near a window and sat down.

"I'll take grilled cheese on wheat, and tea," Anja said to the waitress when she came to us.

"Sounds good to me," I said, handing her the stained menu.

"You want cups or glasses?" The woman's wig was slightly off center and her skin was pale white. She looked down at us with a half sneer that said "I'm looking down on you two."

"American on mine." Anja.

"You too?"

"Yeah."

The woman mean-mugged me, and I threw her my best up-yours smile.

"Michael had this place on the itinerary and I assumed it was Ellen's idea to meet here," Anja said, looking around after the woman strode away. "I'm not sure now."

"It's deliberately out of the way," I said. "She might be afraid of being seen with us."

"This place stinks."

It did. I had smelled something like it before, stale beer and urine settling into weeks-old dirt, vomit and ammonia on weekend mornings, something vile on the stove that needed to be taken off hours ago. There were fifteen other customers, nine guys and six girls. The guys could have been Sturmers, but they didn't have the whole costume. While real Sturmers had retro biker outfits, these guys had only some of the gear, a leather jacket here, a few studs there. Some customers left, others drifted in. It was not a place for a medical technician.

Javier had said he would send Ellen our pictures. It made me feel uncomfortable to know that Javier had my picture to send to anyone.

The place wasn't exactly dark, but the deep-red paint gave it the feel of a funeral home. I wanted to ask Anja how her people cremated their dead, but I didn't want to spook her out.

The grilled cheese sandwiches came, along with glasses of tea.

"We should have ordered wine," I said. "You like wine?"

"I don't know," Anja said. "Never drank any. But my father used to drink a lot. When my parents broke up, he used to take me to bars and get plastered. I thought he was hoping I'd get kidnapped or something."

A nervous-looking woman came in, looked around, and then walked over to the woman who had served us. Nervous Girl was tall, young, and kind of pretty. She wore a short flared skirt and carried a square black-and-silver purse. When the waitress pointed in our direction, I figured Ellen had arrived.

"Here comes our contact," I said to Anja.

She came over, smiled, and took the seat that Anja left when she slid over.

"You must be Dahlia," Ellen said. "I have a friend from the Dominican Republic. She's even darker than you."

What the hell did that mean?

"And I'm Anja," Anja said. "Nice to meet you."

Ellen looked about twenty-two, twenty-three, with a pleasant face. Her hair was combed to one side, and I wondered if that was the way she usually wore it.

"How was your trip?" Ellen asked. Nice voice.

"Uneventful," I said.

"I really don't like flying anymore," Ellen said. "I had some work done on my shoulder and they moved my chip or something. It doesn't register right, and I keep having to go through a body search."

"The weather is nice in Minnesota," Anja said. "I thought it would be cooler."

"There's no humidity to speak of, even though we're near the lake," Ellen said. "Will you be in St. Paul long?"

The waitress came over with her pad and asked Ellen if she wanted anything. She took her order for a white wine and walked away without saying anything.

"I don't think so," I answered. "Are you from here?"

"More or less," she said. "I was in New Jersey briefly after Javier's . . . accident. Then I came back here."

"I got the idea that you were important to him," I said.

"We met at Stanford. We were among a group of wunderkinder they took right out of tenth grade. I was fifteen and he was a little younger, I thought. He was into law and I liked science. I also liked Javier. A bunch. We dreamed a lot of good stuff. Marriage and forever and ever and that kind of thing. It meant everything to me. Not just a lot. Everything.

"Then one day he went out with some frat guys. They

went off campus and they all started drinking. They were horsing around, and one of them picked Javier up and threw him across a table. He felt something go . . ."

She stopped talking, and Anja put her hand on her arm.

"You don't have to continue, Ellen," Anja said.

"He felt something go wrong with his back, but he didn't want to look as if he couldn't hang out with the other guys, so he didn't say anything. He tried driving home alone even though he was in a lot of pain."

"And that's when he had the accident?"

"He was so bitter."

She was crying.

"To me it didn't matter—it mattered, but I still loved him," Ellen said. "You know what I mean?"

"I do."

"He didn't want to see me again after he got out of the hospital." Ellen took a small sip of her drink. "It was as if I represented all his dreams, and none of them could come true anymore."

"You've stayed in touch?"

"He makes sure to keep me away," Ellen said. "I can't talk about us anymore. When he hooked up with Michael, I was so proud of him. He still wanted to make a difference in the world. When I got the job with CTI, it was like we were touching through a glass wall. It wasn't much, but it was something. We were both trying to make a difference."

"What do you do for CTI?" Anja asked.

"Blood work, mostly," Ellen said. "I was involved in the Jack-2 project."

"Which is?"

"We did a lot of work on prostaglandin anomalies," Ellen said. "We started with J-2 and figured a way to alter the composition of the prostaglandin to— Are you into biology?"

"Not at all," Anja said. She seemed a lot more relaxed, even though I hadn't particularly noticed her being uptight before.

"Well, the theory is that things go wrong in the body because the prostaglandins don't work as well as they should," Ellen said. "We were working on the J-2 prostaglandin progressions. They go through these progressions and then, for some reason, the patterns alter, and they're not doing what they're supposed to do. We were working on one progression, the one that alters platelet production, when one of our researchers found the link between the transmitters—the proteins that carry the prostaglandin from one cell to the other—and a bunch of diseases. The two most promising—"

Ellen stopped and looked around the bar. Somebody had changed the music. Too loud, but it wasn't bad.

"Cell growth regulation and cell repair," Ellen said. "We all got excited. I'm excited now, just talking about it. Our people showed the results of the initial tests to some new execs who came in from somewhere. They stopped everything. They just moved the funding back to bacteria analysis, which isn't all that interesting."

"What's the point?" I asked. "You think they just didn't get . . . whatever you were getting?"

Ellen leaned forward until she was less than a foot from my face. "The key is the rate of cell growth. How many platelets are being produced, or how many white blood cells? If you control cell growth and keep it consistent, you can stop most cancers, and you can slow down the aging process until you wouldn't be able to notice it in most people until they reached a hundred and ten or so."

"So why did they stop it?" Anja.

"Because the correction—adjusting the way the cells developed—was a process, not a drug. You don't make money on processes. You make money on drugs. If we found a way to convert the process so that it would work through pills—even fifty percent as effectively—CTI stood to make trillions of dollars!"

"Or a two-percent growth in a year!" I said.

"That's what I wanted to get to Javier!" Ellen said.

"Crap!" Anja clapped her hand to her forehead. "They're looking to make a profit? But who?"

"The two executives who shifted the funding are also on the board of Natural Farming." Ellen downed the glass of wine, then wiped her lips with the back of her hand. "They've been playing a bigger and bigger role for the last year and a half. Almost two years."

"¡Ay, chica! Natural Farming is sneaking around CTI?" I asked.

"Exactly!" Ellen said.

"Did any of the science guys at CTI object?" Anja asked.

"Yeah, we were so excited with the science, with all of its potential." Ellen's mouth twisted as if she were hurting.

Her eyes darted around and then she looked into mine. "But they told us that if any of us ever publicly mentioned the prostaglandin project, we'd be fired and never work again. That's the way it goes in our field. You can never get into a lab without an okay from up above. I thought that, maybe, Javier could help."

Suddenly the crap was coming together. All the players were showing up on the same field and it was beginning to make a foul kind of sense. I wanted to get back to the hotel and do some serious thinking.

"Maybe it will be okay," Ellen went on. "Maybe they'll restore the funding and we'll be back on track. I don't know."

"Anja, if Natural Farming took over CTI, the big C-8 companies would be one giant smaller. Then C-7, or whatever we'd be calling it, could make a fortune—their friggin' two percent—and have even more control of the world."

"These things often take years," Ellen said. I could sense she wasn't getting the bigger picture. "In the end it'll be okay. I think it'll be okay."

"Why were executives from Natural Farming on the board of CTI?" I asked.

"That's the way things work in these big companies," Ellen said. "One person can sit on the boards of three or four companies. It just works that way. Cooperating interests. Where's the bathroom?"

We looked around and I saw a sign that read "Studs" over a door in a corner of the room. I pointed to another door and another sign, which was too far to read. Ellen got up quickly.

"It's all laid out on the memory stick in my purse," she said. "It's everything I know."

"Anja, this is it! Everything makes sense now," I said. "If Natural Farming takes over CTI, then C-8 suddenly becomes C-7."

"And they make their two-percent growth by getting smaller," Anja said. "Not by getting bigger."

"If Ellen's science is right and Natural Farming pulls this off, they'll be able to say who gets old, who dies of cancer, maybe even who catches a friggin' cold!"

"You really think they'd have that much power?" Anja's eyes opened wide.

"Apparently *they* think so!" I said. "Check out her bag."

Anja moved Ellen's purse across her knees and next to her between her leg and the wall.

"You ever see a movie called *Casablanca*?" she asked me.

"What?"

"It's an old movie that takes place in Morocco, same place that Sayeed is from," Anja said, looking in the purse. "Humphrey Bogart was in it. Here's a plastic case marked 'Javier.' It's got to be the memory stick."

"Let's take Ellen back to the hotel," I said.

The waitress headed in our direction.

"You want anything else?"

I noticed a guy from one of the tables standing and heading toward the bathrooms.

"What kind of pie you got?" Anja.

"Cherry, apple."

"I'll take cherry," Anja said.

"Me too," I said as the waitress towered over the table. My view of the bathrooms was blocked for a second as she made a big deal of cleaning the cracked Formica top. I was getting nervous.

"Let's call a taxi now," Anja said when the waitress was gone. "Or do you think Ellen's driving?"

"I don't think a cab is going to pick us up out here," I said. "As soon as Ellen comes back, we can all split."

Me on the phone to Michael. It went to voice mail. Shit!

"Michael, if the information we're getting here is true, everything is coming together. We're still with Javier's contact, and I'll call you later. Everything is falling into place. It's a major power grab."

We waited two minutes. Three. There was a clock on the wall, and the hand moved slowly.

"Anja, what are you thinking?"

"Same as you—what's she doing in the bathroom?"

"Can we get the car back at the hotel to come pick us up?"

Anja on her pad trying to locate the car. Me getting scared and my mouth going dry. I glanced toward the bathrooms. Suddenly a slight man came out from the shadows. He headed quickly toward the front of the café and through the heavy doors. Was there another room in the back, or had he come out of the ladies' bathroom?

"Fourteen minutes unless something happens," Anja said. "The car will be here in fourteen minutes."

I took Anja's pad and saw an area map. The icon for the car was flashing.

"Anja, I think I saw a guy come out of the ladies' room." I was whispering.

Another man got up and went into the "Studs" room. Two minutes later he came out, wiping his hands with a paper towel. He stopped and looked at me and Anja, then threw us a kiss.

I flipped him the bird. He grinned. Good, a normal asshole.

I looked at Anja's GPS screen. The car was getting near.

"I'm going in," I said.

"I'll come with you," Anja said.

"No, you wait out here."

I was wearing new flats but not sneakers. I thought of the bathroom having a tile floor and wished I had worn rubber-soled shoes.

The smell of urine was strong as I pushed the door open. I looked in the mirror and didn't see anybody. Where the hell was Ellen?

I looked down under the doors of the stalls and saw a pair of dark, shiny pumps. I pushed the door open cautiously. Ellen looked up at me. The left side of her face was bruised, and the white of her eye was bloody.

"Ellen, let's go!" I said.

"It's no use." Ellen shook her head. There was snot on her lips, and I grabbed some toilet tissue and wiped at it.

"It won't do you any good to stay here either," I said. "Move it!"

She started to say something, and I grabbed her and pulled her up. She was sniffling and stumbling as I pulled her from the stall. I got her to the door, opened it, and pushed her out. In a minute I was half lifting, half dragging her through the café.

"How did you get here?"

Ellen mumbled something about a friend dropping her off.

Anja moved to Ellen's side and slipped under her shoulder. The other people in the café tensed as we made our way toward the door.

The night air was refreshing, and my breathing was almost normal as the car was pulling up. I tried the door and it was locked. I looked at my phone, found my way back to the GPS app, and opened the door.

Anja pushed Ellen into the backseat and got in with her. I got in the front just as the waitress came out of the Pig's Eye Café with a guy. I didn't think they were up to anything good.

The car started forward with a jerk, and we were on our way.

"I can't stand being hit," Ellen said. "Any kind of physical violence is just . . ."

"It's okay." Anja was trying to calm her down. "It's okay. We're all in this together."

"No, we're not," Ellen said. "They don't know who you are. The guy in the bathroom was asking if you were cops. Me, somehow, he knew. I said you were just friends."

"Have you told us everything you want to?" Anja asked.

"Did you get the memory stick?" she asked. "They'd kill to keep that information hidden. I don't mean literally, but they'd be really pissed."

"How did they know you were coming here tonight?" I asked.

"I don't know," she sobbed. "I just don't know."

I thought of Ellen calling us at the hotel and telling us where to meet her. Her messages were probably being intercepted.

Anja was wiping Ellen's face with tissues and pushing her hair away from her bloody cheek.

"The names of the executives from Natural Farming who are on both boards," Ellen said, "and the names of all the technicians at CTI who worked on the prostaglandin project are on the stick. There are a few other names too. Doctors and nurses we can trust."

"You want us to take you to the police station?" Anja asked.

"No!" Emphatic. Clear. "Just drop me off in front of your hotel. I'll be okay."

"Ellen, we can take you home," I said.

"I'll be okay once I get into my apartment building," Ellen said. "And I've got friends I can call. Really, I'll be fine."

I didn't believe that, but we dropped Ellen off and saw her immediately get into a cab.

"You think they traced us?" Anja asked in the elevator.

"No, they're not that sophisticated," I said. "They can always bully people like Ellen. They probably had her phone tapped and knew about a meeting, but not who we are. That's why they didn't try to stop us outside."

In the room we waited until Ellen had had time to get

home and then called her, but the calls kept going to voice mail. Was she afraid to answer the phone?

I called Michael and told him what had gone down. I could hear him cursing under his breath.

"Send me all the data tonight—or maybe send it to Javier," he said.

"We'll be there by noon tomorrow," I said.

"Send it tonight," Michael said. "Just in case there's a problem."

Like us getting killed before we get home?

The St. Paul–Minneapolis Airport was bustling. Anja cradled a container of coffee between her hands as we sat in the gate area.

"We should get something to eat before we get on board," I said.

"I can't stomach artificial eggs, phony bacon, and those processed potatoes." Anja made a cute face.

"How was the food in Africa?" I asked.

"Okay, if you can stomach everything being overcooked," she answered.

"They can't cook in Africa?"

"You have to overcook the food to make sure it's safe," Anja said matter-of-factly.

"I wonder if we should have made copies of the material Ellen gave us," I started. "If we had copies, we could—"

Suddenly Anja grabbed my arm. She was looking past me, over my right shoulder. She was terrified. I turned and didn't see anything.

"What? *What?!*"

"The television screen."

I looked up and saw the screen. There was an image of Ellen on it, but no sound. The trailer under the image was about something going on in St. Lucia.

We got up and walked quickly to another row of benches, sat down, and got the news up on Anja's phone. It took less than a minute to get to Ellen's story. They were claiming she had jumped from her apartment window.

Twenty-three-year-old Ellen Chaikin, apparently in despair at the prospect of being laid off as a technician at CTI, jumped to her death from her well-appointed fourteenth-floor apartment in downtown St. Paul last evening. Ironically, a spokesman from CTI claimed that they had rescinded the layoff notice just that afternoon, but Miss Chaikin, a lab worker, had not yet been informed.

I was completely spooked. I felt mad as hell and even more guilty. We should have insisted she come to the hotel with us. I wanted to puke.

On the plane. We were nearly numb with the weight of it. Someone we had sat with, had talked with, had hustled out of the café the night before, was now dead. Anja was crying softly, her small chest going up and down as we settled in. The flight attendant brought her a glass of water and I thanked him.

Anja sipped the water, then put her head against my shoulder. "She was murdered!" she said.

"Maybe," I said.

"Dahlia, it had to be murder," Anja said. Her face was close to mine, and it felt good having her this close. "These people are terrible and they're doing terrible things."

"Maybe," I repeated.

Anja moved away and looked at me, puzzled. "Then what?"

"Maybe it was Ellen's way of telling us just how important this takeover is," I said. "Maybe she was saying, 'It's worth my life to let you know how I feel about it.'"

"Oh," Anja said. And after a long while, she said again, "Oh."

16

Morristown. Javier was a mess. His face was puffy and swollen, and I imagined him crying. Him being so upset messed with Anja, too. Dear, sweet Anja. She was the most empathetic person I had ever met. Sometimes it felt creepy the way she understood how I thought, but I loved being with her.

The talk was all about how Javier and Mei-Mei were sure that Sayeed had left Morocco and was somewhere in Florida.

"I estimate that he has close to a hundred people with him," Mei-Mei said. She was back to center stage and confident. But her voice was shaky.

There was no talk about Ellen's death, but I knew it was filling up Javier's head. I wondered if he was thinking of what they'd had going on at one time or how he had walked away from her.

"A hundred guys isn't very much," Tristan was saying. "He's either going to have to sign up local guys or somehow get his hands on some super weapons."

"If we find out where he's headed in Florida, I can check out the local gang scene," Drego said.

"It looks like Miami," Mei-Mei said. "Some of Sayeed's people have rented rooms there."

"Let's say that he is trying to make connections." Michael turned sideways in his chair. "How do we stop him? How many people can we rely on?"

"We can count on about two hundred guys," Tristan said. "We can outgun Sayeed if we need to up the two hundred number. After that it gets hairy. I can call on a bunch of young guys and some girls from around the country who are okay with fighting for what they believe in. Nobody wants to just run up on a beach to get killed."

Tristan was more animated than I'd ever seen him.

"Javier, can you coordinate . . . Javier?"

Javier was losing it again. His head was down, his face in his hands. I tried to imagine him with Ellen, the two of them together.

"I'm okay," Javier managed. "I can bring together whatever resources we have if Tristan gives me the contacts. In fact, I want to bring them together. I'm ready to do it."

"The more we know about what Sayeed's got going on, the better we're going to be," Tristan said. "We don't want surprises."

"Drego, you want to go to Miami? Maybe you and Tristan, so we have two sets of eyes going on?"

"Tristan looks like a cop," Drego said. "He won't function with the people I'm dealing with."

"He's probably right." Tristan. No resentment. He was easing into his element.

"Mei-Mei?" Michael asked.

"*No!*" Mei-Mei's voice was high and sharp. Emphatic. Hard. I imagined her squeezing her legs together. She was out of her comfort zone. "I don't think I'll like Miami."

The porcelain queen was vulnerable after all. I felt almost sorry for her.

"Drego." Michael had a stub of a pencil in his hand and pointed it across the table. "This is your show—can you do it alone?"

A beat. Drego was thinking.

"You down, Dahlia?" Drego asked.

"I'm down," I said.

Across from me, Mei-Mei sat up in her chair; she glanced at Drego, then quickly away.

"I'll work it out," Michael said. "We'll set up in Miami when the time comes. Meanwhile, Drego and Dahlia will be our intelligence team. Javier, you can map out the scene. Tristan will nail down our resources. How about weapons?"

My stomach turned. They were still on the same kick.

"I think we can match Sayeed," Tristan said.

"If I'm right," I said, "if Sayeed is just a pawn that C-8 is pushing up the board, they won't want him to win. They just need him to show up."

Michael seemed confused. I thought back to when he was telling me how he'd put together his band. Get the best, let them work.

Michael, I'm the best you got.

"Mei-Mei, will you and Anja make contact with some doctors or nurses in the area to see if they're available in case we need them?"

"Yes." Mei-Mei spoke softly. "I'm on board, Michael."

"I think . . . I think there are a lot of people who thought like Ellen did," Javier said. "They'll work with us."

"Okay, Javier and I will coordinate the operation and then work with Tristan's people when the time comes," Michael said.

"I think I got Sayeed's style together," Drego said. "I got some maps I made up from Al Jazeera news accounts. We know he's the big man in North Africa," he went on, shuffling through a sheaf of papers. "He's got better players than some of the other groups in those mountains, but he's still old-school and you can figure him out."

Michael, Tristan, and Drego started talking about Sayeed the way you think athletes review tapes of a football team they are going to play. The tension in the room rose.

As the guys talked, they were all getting excited. The room was beginning to smell of sweat. They were talking about Sayeed, about a theoretical encounter, but their body language told me that they wanted to engage, not avoid an encounter. I hadn't expected this. Maybe a little from Drego. Maybe even Tristan, but Michael was into it too. Some macho shit was kicking in, and I suddenly saw what Anja was talking about. They were becoming believers in confronting Sayeed. The focus had changed.

I thought about Ellen saying that Javier just wanted to hang with the frat guys and show he had the right stuff. I wondered if he was doing the same thing this time.

"Sayeed always spreads his people at the foot of a mountain in Morocco," Drego said. "You get this wide line with the mountains and fog as a backdrop; you never know how many people you're going to be fighting. I've read reports where people started running away just looking at his men from across a field.

"He moves forward—is this useful to you, Dahlia? But he attacks from the wings." Drego couldn't wait.

"Where's he in this formation?" Michael.

"In the rear." Drego. "He's coordinating the attack from behind the lines, mostly cell phones, but he makes a show of using falcons and stuff. We think that's just Hollywood."

"No!" I heard myself saying. "We're not talking about a football game, and Sayeed is not the enemy. C-8 is the enemy!"

There was silence. Then Michael spoke.

"Dahlia, we know that C-8 is the enemy. But if they're going to bring Sayeed into this country, with even a hundred of his people, then he's the one we're going to have to fight."

"I think I want to go home and think," I said. "I want to do projections based on what C-8 intends, not just on what Sayeed is doing. Sayeed has to be just another piece of shit to these big corporations. Can't you see that? They don't care any more about this man than they care for the

Sturmers or the poor slobs trying to scrape a living out of the streets. Sayeed cannot be our focus!

"We need to rethink this thing as if we're playing with hard-nosed and *damned* intelligent professionals, not some brown-skinned cowboy out of North Africa!"

More silence. I felt suddenly alone. This was *not* what they wanted to hear.

"If that's what you want," Michael said. His voice was even, flat.

"Dahlia, what's your take on this?" Tristan. "Where's your train going?"

"For a combat situation, there have to be four components for the aggressor. The first is that the target has to be in his area of influence. Miami is *not* in Sayeed's area. Second, he has to see a clear goal. There is no clear goal for a band of Africans in Miami," I said. "He's got to be sure he's going to win. In America? No way! And last, if he's going to start anything, he's got to be sure there's not going to be a kickback he can't handle. None of this fits Sayeed. All of it fits C-8. The world is their area of influence. The goal is more money for their pockets. They always win. They don't expect any opposition. No computer projection is going to make Sayeed the problem!"

Another friggin' silence. At least they were thinking.

Michael said we needed a break and called somebody to get me a lift to the Bronx. I think he was disappointed.

As I checked my rucksack to make sure I had my chargers, Anja came to my side. She put her arm around my waist.

"Michael send you?" I asked.

"Yeah, he thinks all the talk of fighting has got you spooked."

"What do you think?"

"I trust you," Anja said. "You rely on what you have in your head, and you got a lot up there, girl."

She smiled.

"You want to come home with me?"

"Yeah, sure."

I hadn't expected her to say yes, and my face must have shown it. She asked me if I really wanted her to come. I said yes.

The car dropped me and Anja off a little after five. The sky was still a cheery blue, with little wisps of clouds floating in the distance, but somehow the neighborhood looked different.

"Are we in the right place?" Anja.

"Give me a second," I said. Then I saw what had changed. There were now rolls of ugly barbed wire between the houses where I had played as a child and where kids were always running between their backyards and the quiet street. I had been away for a minute, and there were wires coiled angrily from ground level to the eaves. Disgusting.

Mrs. Rosario greeted us, threw her huge arms around Anja, and squeezed her into the warmness of her body.

"Any friend of Dahlia is my daughter too," Mrs. Rosario said.

"Thank you, ma'am." Anja smiled.

"I am so glad you're home!" Mrs. Rosario said. Then she said it again in Spanish. "We'll have a wonderful dinner for you! Do you like stew?"

She was speaking to Anja, who nodded and gave the thumbs-up sign.

"One hour—it's already on," Mrs. Rosario said. "Dahlia, baby, are you too tired to eat?"

"Never too tired to eat with you. Mrs. Rosario," I asked, "what's with the barbed wire?"

"A few kids, maybe *favelos*, maybe not, were wandering around in the yards," she answered. "Probably looking for something to eat. But you never know."

Upstairs to my place. Mrs. Rosario, or someone, had changed the calendar to one that had a painting of St. Cecelia. She was beautiful.

Anja was looking around the room, and I watched her taking in every detail of the old furniture, every picture stuck around the mirror, every yellowed memento.

"What do you think?" I asked.

"Looks like a life," Anja said. "I like that in a person."

"The barbed wire wasn't here before."

"Dahlia, are you discouraged?" Anja asked me.

"Just a little," I said. "At this last meeting, after coming back from St. Paul, I felt as if I was in the middle of the ocean in a storm. There's lightning all around and big waves, and you don't know what to do next. The guys seem to be latching on to facing Sayeed somewhere, but Sayeed isn't the big show, Anja. The big show is still C-8."

"And they're as hard to get at as the ocean," Anja said. "I got you on that. You thinking of saying that we shouldn't go to Miami?"

"We have to go to Miami," I said. "But we need to bring our best minds with us, because we really don't know what we're facing. Figure this—somewhere there are two fat guys with double chins doing computer projections for C-8—"

"You've *seen* them?"

"No, but I want them to be fat guys with double chins," I said.

"Oh, okay, and hair growing out of their noses!" Anja added.

"Right! And they're entering data about Sayeed and how he's going to affect things. I think they're dragging bait through the water to see what happens. But with Sayeed, it's going to be some dangerous bait!"

"Dahlia, Sayeed doesn't look like any show-and-tell to me."

"It's not important what he looks like to you, or to the guys, Anja," I said. "What does it look like to C-8? Whatever they're doing, Sayeed is just another piece of it. Like Ellen was another piece of it. Maybe C-8 had her killed, maybe they didn't, but they sure had some asshole beat her up in the bathroom!"

"You think it's going to get ugly in Florida?"

"Yeah, Anja, I really do."

Anja took the first turn in the shower down the hall. She came back in ten minutes and said that the water was cold and refreshing. I didn't want to take a cold shower, but I didn't want to stink up the place either, so I took my shower next.

The water was cold, and I shared the shower with a spider hanging from a long spider thread. That cheered me up a little.

Down to dinner.

It was *pollo guisado*, simple and good. Mrs. Rosario had invited Rafael; Ramón, the old man who lived on the first floor; a woman I didn't know; and Lydia, the young girl.

"Lydia made the dessert!" Mrs. Rosario said. "Sugar cookies for everybody who cleans their plates!"

Lydia was wearing jeans and a sequined hoodie. She looked over at Anja and me and gave us a half smile.

"So what have you been doing?" The old man jumped right in. "You save the world yet? Because I didn't hear anything."

"Ramón, shut up until I introduce our guest. Anja is a friend of Dahlia's and a friend of mine. Isn't that right, *chica*?"

"Yes, it is."

"And this old man is Ramón, who died ten years ago but is too stubborn to lie down. This is Isobel, a saint. This is Rafael, not a saint. And this is Lydia, an angel. We are lucky in this house to have one saint, one angel, Dahlia, and now you."

"I still didn't hear nothing about the world being saved!" Ramón said.

"You can't even hear the television without blasting it all over the house, Ramón." Mrs. Rosario was ladling out the stew. "If Dahlia saved the world and everybody was talking about it, you would be the last to know!"

"You can't save the whole world at once," I said. "You need to save a little piece at a time. Tonight I'll try to save the chicken stew."

"You need to give the chicken some mouth-to-mouth, but I don't think it's going to help him!" Rafael said. "He looks kind of tired to me."

"Dahlia, Isobel is Ramón's niece." Mrs. Rosario gestured toward the woman, who nodded and smiled at me. "She doesn't tell stupid jokes, but she has a job working for a car service."

"Wonderful," I said.

"What do those boys do?" Mrs. Rosario sat down and handed a large slotted spoon to Ramón.

"First, we have boys and we have girls," I said. "Like Anja."

"Is she smart?" Lydia asked.

I looked toward her and saw that she had her head down.

"Anja's very smart," I said.

"*¿Habla español?*" Head still down.

"I'm afraid not," Anja said.

"But she's been all over the world—Africa, South America, St. Paul—and she does good things," I said.

"And the boys?" Mrs. Rosario.

"Michael is the leader," I said. "He used to have a rock

band. He's kind of rich, and he's dedicated to making the world a better place."

"All rich people say that!" Ramón had made a circle of rice on his plate and was now filling it with stew. "They want to make it better for themselves."

"That's kind of what we're doing," Anja said. "Trying to point out that what's good for the very rich isn't always good for everybody else."

"So it's a band? What do you play?" Rafael was having fun with me. Okay.

"It's not a band and I don't play anything," I said. "I more or less do the math for the group."

"Are there any other girls in the group?" Lydia. Still looking down.

"There's one other girl. Her name is Mei-Mei," I said. "She's very good at chess."

"So she's smart?" Lydia asked.

"All the people in the group are smart, Lydia," Mrs. Rosario said. "Dahlia likes to be with smart people."

"Mei-Mei's very smart too," Anja said. "Like you."

"Lydia is going to make some man a wonderful wife." The woman Isobel agreed with herself by nodding. "She already cooks well. You'll taste her cookies tonight. They're much better than anything you can buy."

"When I was a little girl, my grandmother—who was more of a mother to me than my real mother—told me that if a woman can cook and comb her hair, she'll make a good wife," Mrs. Rosario said. "They used to say that if a woman came out of her house with a wooden spoon and a comb, she was looking for a husband."

"What's the hardest part about saving the world, Dahlia?" Ramón again. "Because if it's easy, I may take it up myself. I need a hobby to keep me young."

"What do you think, Anja?" I asked.

"Figuring out who the enemy is," Anja said. "Sometimes that's hard."

"That's what the boys do," Rafael said. "A boy always knows who the enemy is. You look at a man and the man looks at you, and right away you know if he's a friend or somebody who's out to kill you."

"You could be wrong, Rafael," Mrs. Rosario said.

"How do you know if somebody is smart?" Lydia asked. "Do they give you tests?"

"Smart people kind of recognize other smart people." Anja smiled as she spoke. "Maybe it's a kind of radar. What do you think?"

"Could be." Lydia. Now she was smiling. I liked her more and more.

"A man just has to open his mouth one time to me and I know if he's smart or if he's stupid," Rafael droned on. "Even if he just says hello, I can tell. You got to feel it."

"If you feel sick and you go to a doctor, is he your friend or enemy?" I asked Rafael.

"If he's a good doctor, he's your friend." Rafael was pleased with his answer.

"And if you can't afford him?" I asked.

"Then he's neutral," Rafael said. "To you, he's not a doctor anymore."

I didn't bother answering. Rafael didn't get it and maybe never would.

"This stew is wonderful!" Anja.

"You look like a girl who eats a lot," Ramón, the old man, said. "That's okay in a girl, because you never eat as much as boys do."

"How do you sleep when you're away so much?" Mrs. Rosario asked.

"Michael has this huge house in Morristown," I said. "We all have separate rooms, and they're pretty quiet, so I don't have trouble sleeping. You put chili peppers in this stew?"

"Not enough?"

"I think it's enough," I said. "I just wondered. My mother never liked anything too spicy. There's a lot of flavor in this stew."

"It's the lime juice that brings it out," Isobel said. "She could be a cook in a fancy restaurant. Easy. I mean the kind they have in the big hotels in New York."

"If you could get a job in one of those hotels," Mrs. Rosario said. "Jobs don't grow on trees, you know."

"Maybe the man who takes away your jobs is your enemy," I said.

"Rafael, she has a point," Mrs. Rosario said. "You have stew on your shirt."

Rafael grunted. Perfect answer.

"If you don't know who the enemy is, how can you fight them?" Lydia.

"We know what they do, and we can fight against that," I said. "If you go to a doctor and you can't afford to pay to be treated, you can fight against the high fees."

"You're too young to get sick, Lydia," Mrs. Rosario said. "And Dahlia and her friend—Anna?"

"Anja."

"What kind of a name is that?" Ramón asked. "Is that Jewish? I don't have anything against Jewish people."

"It's Czech," Anja said.

"He's got nothing against Czech people either," Isobel said. "The only people he doesn't like are Germans, Haitians, French because he thinks they're white Haitians, Canadians, Italians, and everybody from the Middle East."

"I don't like Japanese people either," Ramón added proudly.

"Dahlia, do you have sex with the boys?" Lydia.

"Lydia! Oh, my God!" Mrs. Rosario slapped the back of Lydia's head. "You *never* ask that kind of question. . . . Dahlia, I'm so sorry."

"It's all right, Mrs. Rosario," I said. "No, honey, we don't have sex with the boys."

"We don't kiss them or anything," Anja said. "We're all very serious. There are a lot of bad things going on, and we don't have a lot of time to fool around."

"She doesn't mean anything, but today's children are too bold," Isobel said. "When I was a child, we didn't say anything at the dinner table. We didn't even ask for another serving."

"You lived in Brooklyn, Isobel," Ramón said. "When you were young—which wasn't yesterday—things were different. Who can afford to live in Brooklyn now?"

"Dahlia, does Anja like black beans? She's not eating them." Lydia. Again.

"I'll get to them," Anja answered.

"So how much are they paying you?" Mrs. Rosario asked.

"They're paying our expenses," I said. "It's like volunteer work."

"Are you actually going to fight somebody?" Lydia asked. "You're going to hit them?"

"Ladies don't fight, child." Isobel.

"We might fight when we go to Florida," I said.

"You're going to Florida?" Mrs. Rosario asked.

"I don't like Cubans either," Ramón said.

"You don't mean real fighting—she doesn't mean real fighting, Lydia," Mrs. Rosario said. "She means like a debate. Isn't that right, Dahlia?"

"No, the people we'll fight against in Miami have guns," I said. "And we'll have guns."

"Oh, my God!" Isobel. "Oh, my dear sweet God!"

"You don't have to go to no Florida," Rafael said. "You can stay right here. No man lets his woman go fight with guns. That's stupid. You stay right here. Why do you have to go fighting and shooting for some rock star? You tell me that! There's no sense to it. You can stay here and get a husband who'll take care of you. Why do you have to go with this stupid shit?"

"We'll take care of each other," Anja started, but Rafael cut her off.

"What do you know?" Rafael was getting angry. He had his head turned toward me, and I could see the vein in his neck bulging. "You're a white girl and you'll go back to being a white girl when the fighting is over. We're Dominicans. With us it's different."

I listened for a while as Mrs. Rosario told me that it would be all right *not* to go, as once she had told me that it was all right *to* go.

I didn't think Rafael, or for that matter any of them, would fully understand what I had to say, but I had to try.

"Rafael, when I came home this time, I saw the barbed wire piled between the buildings. It was as if the strands of wire were a kind of crazy evilness that had replaced the laughter of the kids who used to play there. It told me things were getting worse for our little neighborhood, and for everybody like us. Either I fight against this, in any way I can, and for any reason I can bring myself to, or I just give up. I feel powerless, and when we feel powerless, we stop trying to find a better way. I know that. You know that.

"The group I'm with is still trying to find that better way. We have our reasons, and sometimes they're not the same reasons, but we each have something we want, and we're ready to fight for what we want."

"What do you want?" Rafael.

"I think I want to wake up on a clear day and see a world full of hope and comfort. A world in which what we want will be private and special and fuzzy and warm or whatever we want it to be. My grandmother had a cup she kept on a special shelf and she'd have tea in it or coffee or whatever she felt like having. Everybody needs a cup like that. It's not a lot to ask, Rafael. Just a little private comfort for everybody.

"What we have to do is to stop the corporations and the political groups who want to tell us what to think, and what we should dream about, or what we should eat or wear, or what should amuse us according to what their accountants are telling them. On one hand, it's not a lot to ask to be free to struggle on our own; on the other, it's affecting the whole world, isn't it?"

"I think you're being foolish, but I wish you luck," Rafael said.

"Thanks, Rafael."

We ate the rest of the meal with the kind of light conversation people save for good food and good friends. I loved it, even though I knew everyone was thinking on some level about what I had said and none of us was comfortable.

Finally, the dinner was over and Mrs. Rosario asked Lydia to bring out her dessert.

Lydia went into the living room and came back with an enormous plate piled high with sugar cookies. She looked at me and smiled, and then the plate fell from her hands and crashed onto the linoleum-covered floor.

"Oh!" Mrs. Rosario cried.

"All this talk about fighting has her upset!" Ramón said as Isobel and Mrs. Rosario started picking up the cookies.

Over coffee, Rafael and Ramón agreed that the Mexican football league was prejudiced against other Latino teams.

Anja asked Rafael if he knew that they played football in the Czech Republic. Ramón said that they might play it there, but they weren't really serious. Anja and I listened to football talk until she was falling asleep.

Upstairs. Text message from Michael.

M: Are you okay? We will need you in Florida.

D: Yes, I'm all good.

Before we drifted asleep, there was a knock on the door. I opened it and it was Lydia. She came in and looked around the room.

"How you doing?" I asked.

"Did you know I was smart?" she said.

"Yes," I said.

Anja hugged Lydia.

18

Florida. It was sticky hot, and two minutes out of the airport, I was beginning to stink. Michael had made reservations for us downtown, but Drego wanted a different place to operate from.

"The people I deal with don't do well with security cameras," he said.

"Whatever." Michael shrugged it off. "We go to our hotel first and make plans."

The drivers at the taxi stand were asking people where they wanted to go. It was clear that if you wanted to go to Gated Miami, they would take you. If you wanted to go anywhere else, you were on your own.

We copped two cabs and went to the Paradise, a hotel-casino overlooking the water. It was beautiful. The outside of the hotel, with its steel- and glass-encrusted concrete, shimmered in the midafternoon sun. Anja said the building looked as if it was moving.

The hotel had a security system like the airport's. You stood near the scanner so they could scan your ID chip while they took your picture, and then you were given a key card, which, I presumed, matched your chip. There were bowls of fruit on the counter, and the vacant-looking dude with the plastic smile told us to help ourselves. Anja, Mei-Mei, and I took fruit; the guys didn't. I hoped they were hungry, and I knew I wasn't going to share my grapes.

"So what's our plan?" Drego cut to the chase.

"First, we need exact times, or as near to them as we can manage, of Natural Farming's plans and of Sayeed's plans," Javier said.

"Wait—if we know that Natural Farming is going to take over CTI, and we can show what it means . . ." Tristan was looking at Michael, not Javier. "Why can't we just expose the whole deal?"

"Because people don't want to believe it's bad for them," Anja put in. "That's the main reason we don't fight back. It's simpler to just close our eyes and hope for the best. We always look for the easy way out. Lose twenty pounds in ten days. Get a college degree in six months. When we face hard problems, things fall apart for us. We lose the innocence that questions what's happening to us and go slouching off to Bethlehem or some other place. It'll be easier for people to deal with if we give them something smaller, something a lot easier to hang on to, like a connection between Sayeed and Natural Farming. . . ."

"Then they'll be open to believing the bigger issue." Tristan finished the thought for her. "I get it."

"What's Bethlehem got to do with this?" Javier.

"Nothing, really," Anja said.

"Can we rely on any of the bloggers?" Mei-Mei.

"If we can make it easy for them," Michael said. "Nobody wants to stick their necks out."

Michael said we had to stay in touch with each other and to report any problems. As we were breaking up, he motioned to me.

"You okay going with Drego?" he asked.

"Yes, sure," I said.

"After this is over, we'll have to find each other," he said. He smiled.

"Yeah, sure," I said again.

What the hell did that mean? *Find each other.* I wasn't lost.

Mei-Mei made a big show of kissing Drego before he and I left for our other locale. I guess that was her way of saying he was her man or something. Witch.

Drego was driving. He was taking us through the streets to a motel that he said the gangs would respect.

"We have to make a stop first," he said.

Drego seemed jumpy, and there were little beads of sweat on his upper lip. He was driving too fast, as if he was pissed, blowing by black teenagers standing around in the streets. One of them pointed a gun at the car but Drego didn't stop. The housing here was six times worse than in the Bronx. We passed rows of stacked shipping containers, painted garish colors and with windows cut into the corrugated tin. This was what was passing for housing here.

Drego was on two phones. I hoped he wouldn't kill us on the way. He went down a narrow street, past a one-legged man sitting in a wheelchair, and stopped in front of a small store.

"We'll get out here," he said.

Drego was on the street. I opened my door and tried not to notice the stench.

"Don't worry, we look the part," Drego said.

We did. He was black and lean, and I was Latina. I could have been his woman. He was back on the phone again, this time giving his coordinates.

"Yeah, yeah." He was talking into the phone and looking around. "Two minutes."

He led me to the corner, took a deep breath, and held up two fingers for me to see. Okay, we were going to be picked up in two minutes. Down the street, a man and woman hustled along pushing a baby in a shopping cart. The man had a limp. It was a third world country with the walking wounded roaming the streets. They stopped and stared at us.

That's what the world had come to, people being scared of each other, people eyeing each other suspiciously even though they didn't have anything to steal. Everything that wasn't in the gated community was up for grabs, even lives.

The couple stood watching us, and I moved closer to Drego. I put my head on his shoulder so it looked as if we had something going on. He smelled like aftershave lotion. The couple moved on, the woman nervously peering behind her as they passed on the other side of the street. From my window in the Bronx, it would have been an interesting scene; up close, it was just sad.

I saw the one-legged guy in the wheelchair roll up to the car. He nodded toward us, and Drego nodded back.

The car that approached us had a body that was nearly rusted through, but the sound of the engine was strong. I held my breath as it pulled up.

"Yo, Slice!" Drego.

Drego threw up a halfhearted black power salute and got in next to the driver. The back door opened and I half slid, half got pulled, into the rear seat. Drego ran his greetings and started laughing. I was sitting on some big black dude's lap. Shit. There was another guy sitting next to us with a sprayer, a sawed-off automatic weapon. I wondered if I was going to live until sundown.

The guy whose lap I was sitting on didn't say boo to me. The only ones who talked were the driver and Drego.

"You meet this Sayeed dude?" Drego.

"Yeah, he talked a lot of shit," the driver, a long-headed guy, answered. "Little Frankie was dealing with him mostly. They hit it off good."

"Who's Little Frankie?"

"He runs West Side," Long Head said. "His father's a police officer."

Lap Guy shifted, and I wondered if he was trying to cop a cheap thrill. I didn't move.

We drove for a few minutes, around one block twice, and then pulled into a driveway. Drego got out. I was glad to get some fresh air.

"Thanks," I said.

"We got to be doing this again, sister," Lap Guy said.

Not anytime soon, I thought.

There was a guy in front of the building. He said something to Drego that sounded like "slap," and Drego raised his hands chest high and a little away from his body. The guy frisked Drego quickly but thoroughly. Then he came to me.

"Slap!"

I raised my hands and he went over my body. Then he stood aside, and the door opened. *Typical gang stuff*, I thought.

Inside, the scene was like an old master painting, except instead of some beautiful Italian chick in robes, with the sun coming through the window, and fruit and a silver bowl on the table, there was a dingy room with red shiny drapes and lacy curtains that could have been either off-white or beige. What gave the room its old master look was a hard yellow light that came from a corner lamp. It was a reading lamp that formed a conical beam, bathing the gloomy-assed room in gold. The tacky chairs around the table were old and not too sturdy-looking.

The room smelled like tobacco, or maybe tobacco and air freshener. Either way, I felt like puking. The guy who had searched us pointed to two chairs, and we sat down. I wanted to know what Drego thought about this, but I didn't want to ask him. I did ask myself why I wasn't scared when I thought I should be. Then it came to me that this was all a little lame. The dude who had searched me was real enough, but the scene, in a shabby room like this, was surreal. When another black guy and a girl came in and sat at the table, I wasn't expecting much. The guy was light-skinned, good-looking, with really neat cornrows. He was dressed casual, but his clothes were tailored. Good cut, good style.

The chick was a step-down. She might have been young once, but it was hard to tell when.

The guy was smoking a blunt and offered it to Drego. Drego took a puff and passed it to me, and I just passed it to the chick.

"You don't indulge?" the girl asked. Skinny brown-skinned girl looking out of a pimply face through shiny eyes.

"Not when I'm working," I said.

She smiled. Bad teeth. Crack hag.

"Thanks for letting us drop by," Drego started. "You got my message. What's happening on your end?"

"This guy Sayeed is coming in, dealing heavy paper," Cornrows said. "He's getting everybody's attention and talking about bringing some power to the streets. You know, you can rap all you want, but if the backbeat is pure Benjamins, you going to get some ears perking up."

"Word." Drego.

I was supposed to be paying attention, but instead I was stumbling around Dante's circles looking for an exit. Cornrows was running his mouth about the money that Sayeed was passing out and how everybody was lining up to get their palms covered, and the crack hag was fumbling through her works! She was flicking her needle with her index finger right there in front of me. I was busting my eyeballs trying to blink them back into my head, and she was flicking the end of the needle.

Girl, don't tell me you are going to shoot up in front of us!

Drego was steady on Cornrows' case, like that fat detective on reality television, pumping questions a mile a minute. Cornrows glanced at the girl and then made a gesture like "the hell with it," and he kept running his mouth to Drego.

She was skin-popping, injecting herself under the skin. I was thinking she either couldn't find a vein or she was still kidding herself about having a light chippy. Either way, the voice in her mental GPS was lying to her.

Out on the street again. Back in the same car. On the dude's lap. He fondled my breast and I moved his hand.

"You'd be nice to play with," he said in my ear.

I didn't answer.

"What do you think?" Drego asked. We reached our car and Drego laid some green on the one-legged man who was watching it for us. We were driving again and I resumed breathing.

"He's light, she's sick, and these people are primitives," I said.

"Put that down in your game book," Drego said. "They've been doing this shit for fifty years. In the nineties, they were steady pumping guns into the ghettoes, building low-level mini-armies, and letting us shoot up each other. They're still doing it. You're not going to find any *favelos* anywhere in the country with sophisticated weapons.

"You can control primitives. They think they got power because they got bows and arrows, or slingshots, or Glocks . . . whatever, but any weapons can be taken back whenever the man, or the army, or C-8, or whoever else is in charge wants to take them. All they got to do is to balance the weapons they let them have with the amount of drugs they let them have, and everything remains static."

"What about Sayeed?"

"Sayeed is just another punk with a name and a half-assed rep," Drego said.

"The guy back there said he was dealing a lot of cash," I said.

"My grandfather once said to me that when blacks were segregated, the police, they didn't bother black businesses." Drego turned up a street and sped past some guys huddled around a garbage can on a corner. "You could have a few dollars in your mattress, but you couldn't buy anything. You couldn't buy a boat because you wouldn't have any place to put it. You couldn't buy a house unless it was in the ghetto. You couldn't buy a diamond watch unless it was worth half of what you had to pay for it. Sayeed is showing big money, but it won't do him any good. That's why all the dope dealers used to get caught. They couldn't spend their money, so they showed it off and got busted. Sayeed hasn't learned that yet."

"So you're not scared of Sayeed?"

"Yeah, I'm scared of him," Drego said. "He's paying the brothers in the city with paper, and they're paying him with some phony power. Power will get your ass higher than crack any day of the week."

"I guess." I was already trying to figure out a way to include what Drego was saying in my computer model.

"We're just driving around?" I asked. I was seeing the same places.

"Got to make sure we're not being followed."

"What if we are?"

"Then we give up more information than we have to," Drego said.

"How did you get into swinging with Michael?" I asked.

"Everybody wants the same thing," Drego answered. "We all want respect, a good life, and whatever else makes it on television. If we can't get top tier, we go for second. If we can't get second, we go for whatever we can get our hands on. Sometimes it gets down to fighting in the gutter for crumbs. I was fighting a step up from the gutter. When Michael called, he offered me the same fight I was already dealing."

"But on a higher level."

"Something like that—hey, who's that girl over there?"

He slowed the car down. There was a person on the corner, small in the light from a lamppost. It could have been the crack hag we had just seen. Or another one.

"Get in the back," Drego said. "Quick!"

I climbed over the back into the small rear seat. Drego stopped the car a few feet from the girl. He got out quickly and walked around the front. As she turned, he swung at her. I couldn't believe it! He grabbed her off the ground and headed toward the backseat. I unlocked the door, and in a heartbeat there was a body across my lap.

Drego was in the front seat and we were moving again.

"Keep her head down!" he said.

I pushed her head between my legs and clamped down. She was whimpering, and I felt like shit. What were we doing?

Anja said that all the players in C-8 were true believers. They thought they deserved everything they got and the rest of us were holding them up. Was this what we were doing? Were we becoming true believers and saying it was okay to treat people like dirt?

We drove for two minutes until we got near an empty lot. Drego stopped the car, pulled the girl's head up, and pulled her face close to his.

"Who does Pretty Boy work for?" he asked. "Who's the guy Sayeed is dealing with?"

"What?" she was asking. Only it came out "Wha?"

"Who the fuck is Pretty Boy dealing for?" Drego said again. "I ain't got all night. She's going to kill you if you don't give it up."

The girl twisted her head as much as she could with Drego holding her by the jaw. When she turned her face toward me, I saw it was the same chick who was shooting up before.

"Conrad," the girl mumbled.

"Conrad Butler?" Drego. "And don't lie or she'll shoot you."

"Yeah. Really." She was twisting again, obviously scared, trying to see what I was doing. I slid my hand behind my back.

"Get rid of her." Drego.

I opened the door, and she started moving away from me. I put my foot on her back and pushed her. Drego had the car moving as she hit the ground.

"Conrad Butler is from Atlanta. He took over half the South when things were getting dicey around five years ago," Drego said. "Get in the front again so dudes don't think I'm pimping you."

"How?"

"Blackouts," Drego said. "Anybody who stood up against him got killed along with their whole families. He's a total scumbag."

"I mean how am I going to get back in the front with you driving like a friggin' maniac?"

He stopped. I got over the backseat into the front, scraping my belly on the headrest. There had to be a better way of seeing Florida.

The "hotel" on Fairway Drive looked more like a maximum-security prison than a place to spend a night. It was gray and forbidding. The iron bars on the pretend balconies were rusted and bent. We went in, and a woman with short red hair shuffled over to where we were standing.

"You got to show some ID," she said, pointing to a scanner on the counter.

Drego lifted the scanner and moved it to his shoulder. The woman pursed her lips and nodded approvingly.

"Most people who check in here don't have their chips anymore," she said.

Upstairs to the third floor. Down the hall to 367. Drego slid the key card through the lock and pushed the door open.

It could have been worse. It was musty and smelled of tobacco, but the bed was made. There was a hot water heater on a small desk—maybe it was a coffeemaker—and a plastic ice bucket. The bathroom was dingy, with a toilet seat I wouldn't have been comfortable standing on in high heels.

Drego was back on his phones in a minute. How he talked on two phones at the same time was beyond me, but he did. I powered up my gear and saw that I had nine messages. Six were from people trying to sell me something, and three were from Anja.

A: Dahlia, check out the inflow on careyblog.lee.edu. Half the lines are from yours-very-truly.

I went to the blog site, which I knew was a stupid, right-wing, racist one. There were a bunch of entries about how some black baseball player couldn't read, a few about his white wife who was dyslexic, and a couple about his dog being gay. It would have been funny if these people, like Anja said, weren't true believers and serious about their rants. I was wondering why Anja wanted me to see these, but then I came across a post that maybe Natural Farming was going to grow hashish in North Africa and that was why they were connected to the splibs.

"Drego, did you see this?" I asked. "Anja told me to check it out."

He was looking at something on his smartphone. He checked my screen out and was surprised.

"Anja hacked into their site?" he asked. "I haven't heard black people being called splibs for years."

I scrolled down and there were more rants against the ballplayer, and a lot more against his dog, and more posts about Natural Farming and Africans. Some of them, like the first ones, talked about hash plantations. Anja, and whoever was working the media with her, was kicking it.

D: Who did the posts about the dog being gay?

A: A creepy crawler who probably wanted to get it on with the dog.

Anja sounded upbeat. I felt miserable. At first I didn't know why. The misery of a hotel room didn't bother me that much, so I knew it was something else. I looked over at Drego, and he was working the phones again. I imagined him doing it in Detroit with a bunch of hoochie mamas surrounding him.

"Drego, how long are we going to stay here?" I asked.

"I'm trying to track down one more guy," Drego said. "He's got a head on his shoulders and owes me from the old days."

"Owes you money?" I asked. "I thought Sayeed was flooding the place with money?"

"He owes me his life," Drego said. "I had a reason to kill him and I didn't."

I hoped that was drama.

"What do we need from him?" I asked.

"To find out who Sayeed is sure of and who's sitting on the bench waiting to see which side to come down on," Drego said. "Sayeed doesn't know enough to move into a different territory, let alone a different country, and get everybody to line up on his side. We find who's most paranoid, who's getting the most spooked, and we can work it."

I got back on my tablet and tried correcting one of my earlier models. I had been starting Sayeed off with weak ties. But if he was spreading money around, then there had to be a stronger trail back to its source. I texted that to Anja. Then, against my instincts, I turned to Drego. Something had been bothering me and I had to let him know.

"You—we—didn't have to be so brutal to that girl," I said.

"You feel bad about it?"

"Yes, I do."

"Good." Drego was punching in numbers on his phone. "Sometimes people are so far out of the loop that there's no basis for logic, and no time to be teaching them shit

about what's good for them. You can't reason with somebody when dope takes over their life. I didn't feel good
about adding to her misery either."

"You seemed fine with it," I said.

"I wasn't," Drego answered. "Maybe a little too used to
it, though. But I felt bad. When you stop feeling bad about
hurting people, then you're in trouble. Until then, you do
what you got to do."

Bullshit. Or, at least, maybe bullshit. Was this the way it
really worked? You kept telling yourself that whatever you
did was friggin' okay because it was you and your heart
was good, because when you asked yourself, you came
back with the answers you wanted to hear? I looked at
myself in the mirror and saw that my eyes were puffy and
my cheeks shiny with dried tears. Would makeup cover
that shit?

Could makeup cover the shit of the world?

"Drego, how can you live with yourself?"

"Dahlia, I look at myself real hard to see if I can see a
soul. When I find it, when I see it's not a mask or some
kind of symbol—I move on," Drego said. "It's like my soul
is a shining star. I leave people, I step on people, I hit people who need to be cradled and loved, and I move on. It
ain't easy, girl."

I knew.

Back to the models. I looked at them and they were like
little graphs I had worked with in elementary school. I
switched to time-lapse projection and watched the red and
blue dots move slowly through the graphs. The red dots

were Sayeed's people, and the blue ones were the locals. What Drego was saying seemed right. If Sayeed couldn't depend on all the locals, he would have to change his plans. But I didn't think he would. He was a creature of habit.

"Yeah! Yeah!" Drego was on his feet, snapping his fingers at me. Then he made a motion that he wanted something to write with.

I tossed him a notepad with a keyboard, and he put it on his lap as he held the phone between his cheek and shoulder. He typed furiously for two minutes, then signed off.

"There's nobody buying too heavy into Sayeed's program," Drego said. "Everybody I'm talking to is pumping *me* for information. They want to know what the deal is, and they're in as much of a hurry as we are. Sayeed's supposed to make his move sometime Wednesday."

"That makes sense," I said. "If he grabs the headlines Wednesday, then Natural Farming can make the acquisition announcement Friday and there won't be any business blogs over the weekend."

"And by Monday, it's all postmortem time," Drego said.

"Did you send that information to Michael?"

"No, I'll leave that to you so you can earn your brownie points," Drego said. "Then let's get this place cleaned up. I got a guy coming here in about five minutes with some information."

"Get it cleaned up? This place is like a toilet with a television and a desk, Drego," I said. "What are you going to clean up?"

Drego thought for a second. "Put all your gear in sight," he said. "He thinks I'm operating big-time, and he's going to want to see signs. And if he asks you anything, I hope you got your shit together, because he's no dummy."

"*My shit?* Just worry about your own shit, okay? I know what I'm doing."

I put my tablets and two phones on the desk, and Drego put his two phones, with the screens lit up, on one of the end tables. I didn't know how that was going to impress anybody.

The room was dingy and musty. Dusting it wasn't going to help. The window I was going to open was nailed shut. The rug had a dark stain that could have been blood, and the paint was peeling around the light switch. Wonderful.

My stomach was hurting a little, but the thought of the filthy john turned me off, so I just sat down and mean-mugged Drego. He asked me what my problem was.

"If you can't see it, you should be able to smell it," I said.

A couple of minutes passed and there was a knock on the door. Drego produced a gun from somewhere—it looked like a Glock—and asked who it was. He flattened himself against the wall as he was talking.

Thanks for looking out for me.

"Count!" came the answer.

Drego opened the door, and a big fat guy came into the room. His shirt was open, and you could see the scar across the front of his throat under a gold crucifix. A little greasy dude came in, looked around the room, and settled on a chair. He either had a real bad tumor or he was packing a gun under his left arm.

"What's happening?" Drego.

"You the man!" Count. They exchanged daps and bumped shoulders.

"It's been a minute since I laid eyes on you," Drego said. "What you up to?"

"Trying to get the underground on this Sayeed dude," Count said. "This your bitch?"

"Yeah." Drego winked. "She keeps things tight for me."

Count put one cheek of his fat ass on the table. "You thinking he might be running a game?"

"Everybody's running a game," Drego said. "I think he's just playing the field, seeing where the happenings are. He can't last in no Miami, but the thing to worry about is, what's he going to leave behind?"

"I don't get what he's after," Count said. "He's flashing mad-ass money, they grow the best bye-bye in the world where he comes from, so what's his shtick?"

"They're setting up a performance for him," I said. "He shows up, he grabs some big headlines—big enough for everybody to overlook the real stuff that's going on—then they feed him to the wolves."

"Yo, Drego, she know what she talking about?"

"Yeah, she squeezes out some juice," Drego said. "Any buzz about what Sayeed's looking for?"

"The talk is that he's packing up printers to take back to Africa," Count said. "That don't make no sense to me."

"Printers?" Drego looked at me and shrugged.

"Drego, it makes sense big-time," I said. "They've got to be the latest three-dimensional printers. Whatever you can draw, they can reproduce. All you need is a generator, the raw materials, and some simple machine tools—a metal lathe, a robotic mill, and some way to fabricate circuit boards. In Israel they're making artificial limbs. There's even talk about fabricating organs using the same techniques. With a small roomful of equipment, you can make as many guns, bullets, or anything else that's mass-produced as you want. For a guy who's semi-isolated, it's a dream come true.

"And if Sayeed hooks up with the right technicians, he can download unbelievable weapons. He won't have to come out of the mountains for any supplies," I went on. "It'll solve all his supply problems for years."

"She for real?" Count.

"Yeah, she's for real," Drego said.

"Okay, so he's just in this mess for his take." Count rubbed the middle of his forehead with a stubby finger, then looked at it. "And he's using everybody else."

"You got that," Drego said. "How did you find out about the printers?"

"They keep seeds in a warehouse downtown, and one of my people saw a limo pull up to it and this Sayeed sucker pops out with some fay boys," Count said. "The same stuff that keeps the seeds dry keeps weed righteous, so we're always in there stealing enough to keep our thing going. So we seen boxes with scanning stencils. Scan them with the phones and we know what we know. Maybe we'll go back and take a few printers and see what we can do with them."

"You hold off for two or three weeks?" Drego.

"Ain't no big thing—we don't need guns," Count said. "But you here in Miami, so what you want from me?"

"I need to know who's got Sayeed's back."

"Nobody but some punk Little G's," Count said. He lifted his cheek and farted. "Don't mean nothing to nobody except their mamas."

"Solid."

"Yeah, look, I got to get into the wind." Count stood. "Yo, man, you in love or can I cop some of sweet thing here?"

"No hard feelings, but . . ."

"Yeah, well, if you ever get tired of her, send her down my way."

When Count and his greaseball left, I was relieved.

We checked out, found the car, and drove to the headquarters hotel.

"Drego, you roll tough downhill," I said. "But as far as I'm concerned, it sucks big-time."

"Are you going to tell me that people shouldn't be living like that?" Drego asked. "Running gangs, smoking crack, making violence part of the community dialogue? Are you saying that, or are you just saying you don't want to see it?"

I didn't answer.

Me thinking about what Count had said about just a bunch of wannabes backing up Sayeed.

"The way Count put it, just a group of kids coming in with Sayeed—"

"Nine kids with automatic weapons can wipe out a

neighborhood in thirty minutes," Drego said. "Just because they're young doesn't mean a thing except that they don't know about dying yet. Give a fool an automatic weapon, maybe fifty to a hundred rounds, and you got dozens of people killed. Take fifty kids who don't really know what dying is all about and let them hold some automatic weapons, and you can kill a thousand people. You're trying to make the world a better place for some future time. These kids don't believe in no future. What do you think all the *favelos* are about? You coming down off your high horse, or should I say your isosceles triangle, yet? Because it's time to get real, baby."

Maybe, I thought. Or maybe it's time to find out what "real" means.

19

We were back at the Paradise hotel. When you walked in, you had to pass through security. Huge, ugly suckers packing heat. Drego was on the phone again and headed for the elevator without saying anything to me. I dragged ass behind him and signaled that I had something to say.

"What?!" he asked, covering up the phone.

"I'll have a game plan and a tablet model in the morning," I said.

"Have it tonight," he barked at me. "Ten o'clock."

The macho crap kept coming at me, kept pissing me off, but I gave him the thumbs-up sign anyway. I felt like the bitch on the back of the motorcycle, and I didn't like it.

I had to stop for a minute. The first floor of the hotel

was a casino. I looked around me. It was like a bad art installation. Hundreds of colored lights moving around the gaming machines, the weird noises the machines made—they sounded like cartoon animals making out. There were more old people around than I thought there would be. They were kind of freaky. I knew that wasn't right, but that was me.

People sat in front of the machines. They put in coins and pressed a button to see if they'd won anything. The machine made some noises and then told them that they'd lost. It was pathetic. I focused in on one woman and saw she was spacey. She didn't know where she was or what she was doing. She wasn't really alive or really dead, just in the waiting zone.

These were the High Gaters, with guards and security beams and alarms to keep the bad people in line. Not like my family, Low Gaters, with only pathetic little fake wood fences and statues of the Virgin Mary in front of every house to keep us safe. Oh, yeah, and the barbed wire. I didn't want to become a Low Gater, or a High Gater. I just wanted to have a life.

"Cocktail, dearie?" A waitress offered me a drink from one of six she was carrying around on a tray. She was wearing what looked like a bunny outfit. It could have been a rat suit, I don't know.

Upstairs. Javier greeted me and told me that Anja was in the next room. I didn't know why he was telling me this, but I went in and found her. She was sitting in front of a tablet, in her shorts and a T-shirt with birds printed on the front. She looked cute. She had a plate in front of her. On the plate was a huge cheeseburger, and I realized that I was starving. But this was so different from what I'd just been through. Food, and birds, and people with the same ideas that I had, or maybe just the same hopes. How many worlds were there?

"Can I have a bite?" I asked Anja.

"There's another one over there on the desk," she said. "Help yourself."

I saw the serving tray and the aluminum cover over the plate. I lifted the cover and found the cheeseburger next to a bed of fries. There was a small bowl of some kind of salad next to the plate.

"How did it go?" Anja asked me.

"Mmmfh!" I answered. My mouth was full, and I wanted to get more in it as soon as possible.

"Is that bad or is that good?" she asked, smiling. Home girl, all the way.

I pointed to her tablet and made a circular motion with one finger. "What are you doing?"

"Still organizing the lies," she answered. "I've got a fake network going of people denying the rumors about C-8 not really being connected to Sayeed."

"Details," I said. The cheeseburger was awesome. I had grease all over my lips and something sticky on my chest.

"If I get enough people denying the rumor, then people are going to start believing that it was true," Anja said.

"People know about C-8's connection with Sayeed?"

"No, but they know about the"—she checked a counter on her tablet—"four thousand and nine messages saying it's not true."

"That's what you do all the time?" I asked. "Deal in truth and lies?"

"That's all you need, I think," she replied. "How did your day go? Did Drego turn you into a ghetto chick?"

"I think everything I thought I knew about the world was wrong," I said. "I went into the black section of Miami tonight. It looks like it's been bombed for about six months straight. Met with some people who know about Drego. They've got a lot of respect for him down here. We met with one of the local gang bosses and his girl. Maybe his girl, I don't know. Anyway, she tipped into the room, and then she took out her works and shot herself full of dope right in front of us! Can you believe that?"

"Right in front of you?"

"Yeah!"

"Weird."

"No, not weird—just like there's no real life left for some of these people," I said. "Where did you get the cheeseburgers? Room service?"

"Javier's hooked up with a guy." Anja was working the tablet furiously. "He got food for us. Javier ordered something funky, like lobster Oldburg or something like that. I wouldn't eat a lobster."

"Why?"

"They're ugly," Anja said.

"What are you typing?"

"I'm getting on my mad voice about the rumors," Anja said. "I'm saying that it's people on the left who are spreading them."

"That's a lie too, right?" I said. "It's just us?"

"It's just me, mostly," Anja said. "But more people are coming online and registering their complaints. A lie is a terrible thing to waste."

Wild. The girl who could tell if anybody else was lying could lie like a champ. Loved it.

Copping some downtime. I got my room assignment from Anja and a key card. I found the room and fell across the bed. The whole Miami scene was depressing me. I finally knew why people didn't fight back against C-8, or why they hadn't fought back against dictators in the past. The shit was just too hard.

I almost fell asleep, but I kept thinking about the girl we had dragged into the car. Somewhere, somehow, I was going to have to figure out what her life was about. Then I was going to have to find her and explain it to her.

Knock on the door. I got up because I thought it was Anja. It was Michael.

"How's it going?" he asked.

"Okay. Drego knows some pretty scary people," I said. I moved aside and let him into the room.

"What do your models say?" Michael asked as he sat on the edge of the bed.

"None of them look good," I said. I sat on the bed next

to him and flipped open the laptop. I searched through the files until I found the ones modeling Sayeed's probable attacks, and scanned them. "So far they all show a lot of killing, not that many variations, and C-8 coming out the winner in all of them."

"You going to come up with something different?"

"I'm going to try," I said. He shifted slightly so that our legs were touching. I looked up at him and he moved his leg away.

No, Michael, I can't switch between worlds that easily.

"You look like you could use some sleep," he said.

"Sounds good," I said. "Drego wants my models in"— I checked the time—"forty-five minutes."

"Yeah," he said. "I'll see you later."

To sleep, to dream, and there's the fucking rub.

20

Back to the tablet. Look at the models. Look at the rules I laid out for Sayeed, and the ones for Drego. The most probable scenario, by about 16 percent, was that Sayeed would attack exactly as Drego had thought. He wouldn't vary even if he knew Drego's people were waiting for him. It had worked for him in Morocco, and he would stick with it.

Looked at the maps of Miami. The city was divided into three large sections: gated communities with subdivision names like Garden of Eden and Jalel Valley; the Casino section that stretched from the waterfront to a position almost abutting the Gaters' section; and then the rest of the city, where the poor lived.

The poor section was itself divided into two sections, with a row of low but dense shrubbery separating them. I ran the maps through again to see which of the two outside lanes Sayeed could take to most effect. I picked one with only a slightly better possibility of being right.

Ran everything again, finally realizing I wasn't inputting anything different and would come up with the same results. The phone rang. Drego. There's a meeting in Michael's suite on the third floor.

"Five minutes," he said.

He said it like he was giving me an order. I thought of the girl he had hit in the street. Maybe that kind of crap turned Mei-Mei on. I didn't go for it.

Michael's room. There were about forty guys, all white, in the room. I looked again and saw that some of the guys weren't white, but they looked white, even the black ones. Like a football team. They were mostly built, some of them were good-looking, all serious as shit. Michael was talking.

"Each of you has a squad of eight fighters. I hope it doesn't go that far, but we need to interrupt Sayeed's grandstanding and the buzz it can create. The intelligence, from Drego and Dahlia, is that Sayeed is looking to make a move early Wednesday morning, most likely before the sun comes up. Drego will be in overall command and will lay out the plans for you. If Sayeed does have a lightning force, a unit going from spot to spot to disrupt the fighting, it'll be Tristan's responsibility, and the guys he has with him, to neutralize that threat. Drego?"

"There are three ways into the inner city," Drego started. "We can't be sure which way he'll try or if he'll try to come in all of them. Dahlia, do you have an opinion?"

"In the past he's attacked on the sides, so I think he'll continue that operating method," I said. My throat was going dry. "The tablet model suggests one of the entries over the others as being the most advantageous to him. But if he doesn't trust his foot soldiers, then he's liable to send them in the riskier way, and save his own guys—the guys from Morocco—for the better one."

I looked around the room. They weren't following me! I realized that the projections I was making didn't make sense to them. They wanted clearer answers than I was giving them. No, not clearer, simpler.

"People, these are video-game examples. In the best-case-scenario breakdown, people are going to die. People are going to be blown away and end their lives not knowing what happened to them. Everything we know, or find out, or guess correctly, is just going to make it more likely that we survive."

"That works for me, Dahlia," Tristan said. "Sometimes survival is all you got going for yourself."

"We'll go to the sites Dahlia has mapped out and take a look," Michael said.

21

"Check this out! Check this out!" Mei-Mei's voice went up three tones. We were gathered around Javier's van in the Belle Harbor section. Javier had put a television monitor on the tailgate.

On the screen, a pale-looking man with a big head was talking to a group of younger men and a young woman to his left.

"Who is he?" Drego.

"Florida's lieutenant governor," Javier answered. "I wonder what he's up to."

The woman came up, whispered something to the lieutenant governor, and then stepped back.

After a voice-over announced who he was, Lt. Governor

Adrian Rogers smiled into the camera and relaxed his shoulders. "This afternoon I spoke to the board members and the executive committee of Natural Farming. There have been some fairly persistent rumors about some bizarre connection between Natural Farming, one of the oldest companies in North America, and some black terrorist group from North Africa. I've known Tom Pettaway over at Natural for more than thirty years. He's a good family man, a Marlins fan, and he supports the Seminoles. What more can you ask for? The rumors aren't true, so I asked what Tom and the board made of them."

He wiped the beads of sweat away from his upper lip with his hand as he went on.

"He was straight up with me, as I fully expected him to be. And he pointed out something that we can all take home with us today. Which is that anybody can say that they don't want people going hungry in their country, but it's another thing to actually implement a plan to end hunger throughout the world. Natural Farming is a very well-respected American company. An American company that proposed, merely proposed, holding a demonstration in North Africa. In six months, the company would turn what had been a country on the brink of starvation into a food exporter. That's quite a turnaround, if you ask me. In the wake of this offer—one that has been tentatively accepted by the Moroccan government, by the way—several groups have claimed that they, and not Natural Farming, first came up with the idea.

"In a way, I guess that a terrorist group taking credit

for something a democratic company is doing is a compliment. Natural Farming won't and can't partner with any group or organization that has terrorist ties or even a shaky reputation. I only hope and pray, for the sake of the people of Morocco, that this group has the decency to distance itself from Natural Farming and allow the people of the African region they claim to represent a path to the kind of living they truly deserve. The good people of Florida have nothing to fear from this group and certainly nothing to fear from Natural Farming. My office will issue a press release later giving more details. Thank you."

Rogers turned quickly away from the camera, and the two men who had been standing behind him began handing out a written statement. He didn't take questions.

"He's sealed it!" Anja said. "He's publicly denied the connection between Natural Farming and terrorists but established the connection between Natural Farming and the North Africans! No one is going to believe that load of crap."

"You thinking we can pack it in?" Michael asked. "If people are making the connection between Natural Farming and Sayeed—and they are—I don't think C-8 will have the balls to think they can sneak a takeover past the public."

"They'll just wait a few weeks and try something else," Tristan said. "Maybe run a game about how much they're helping the Moroccans."

"Then we'll go after them again," Michael said. "But the important thing is that we don't have to get into a street battle and end up killing a lot of people."

"Yo, Michael, how the hell do you think Sayeed is going to react?" Drego asked. "You're looking at what Natural Farming is thinking and what you're thinking, but what about Sayeed? Us pushing Natural Farming to back down leaves Sayeed high and dry. If he just folds his tents and walks away, Natural Farming doesn't have to give him nothing, and maybe they'll even get some local police to mess with him. He's got nothing to gain by walking away. They just forced him to make a move—what did Mei-Mei call it?"

"Zugzwang," Mei-Mei chimed in. "He's got to make a move. If he's cut off from Natural Farming and has to go home empty-handed, he's going to lose face in Morocco. If he acts on his own, he's taking a big risk of being ineffective, but he's got to do something."

"I don't think so." Javier. "What's he got to gain?"

"He's been promised three-dimensional printers," I said. "And he needs to maintain his reputation as a badass. Right now, all he sees out there is Natural Farming walking away from him. He doesn't just want the alliance, he *needs* it."

Silence.

The van door opened and a blond boy stuck his head out and said that there was some movement along the upper park line, about a mile and a half away.

"Call Sayeed's phone and see what you get." Javier took a quick glance at Michael. "If his phone is on at all, it will react by connecting with a tower, maybe even two or three towers. We can trace that within a few hundred yards."

"There's lot of interference . . . ," the blond boy started.

"Do it!" The veins in Javier's neck began to throb.

There had been interference all afternoon, and we were sure that C-8 was messing with the radio signals for the Internet. Javier sent out the strong signal and watched his monitors.

"You think he's actually going to attack?" Michael.

"You betting that he won't?" Drego shot back.

I could see the doubt on Michael's face. I felt it too. It would have been easier to believe that the problem had been solved.

Tristan told us to grab some cover just as Blond Boy returned. He said that there were two groups on the move. One was coming toward our position, and the other was moving left.

I was feeling sick. An armored vehicle pulled up. Its camouflage was light and medium brown. Desert disguise, but we were in Miami. The vehicle stopped, and the gun mounted on its rear moved menacingly from left to right. It looked like some huge robot animal. I thought of a praying mantis.

My stomach turned, and things seemed to slow down around me. Javier beckoned me over, and I watched as he powered his wheelchair into the back of the vehicle.

I didn't want to go in, but I didn't want to stay outside either.

The combat command van was dark except for the orange light that bathed the interior sides. The dials were all weird green. Javier lit up a computer screen, and I saw the layout of the area. It was fantastic, a combination of a map projection and photographic images.

"I can direct things from in here," Javier said. "You can help if you want."

"How do you feel?" I asked as the driver pulled a lever and closed the rear hatch.

"As if I want to do something about Ellen," Javier said. "Something personal. Something with a lot of violence."

"I don't think I should be in here," I said. I was thinking again. Nervous, but thinking again. "It doesn't seem real. I don't want to confuse the reality of this scene with a computer projection. This isn't a game."

"In a way . . ." Javier's voice trailed off. I thought he was going to say that in a way it was a computer game. I was feeling that too, and I didn't like the feeling.

"Kevin." Javier touched the driver's shoulder. "Get the door. Dahlia's leaving."

It was harder to breathe outside than it was in the van. The air was heavy with humidity. In the distance, the morning sun played along the edges of the squat buildings, bending the rays so that the outlines of the decrepit housing lost their shape. I saw Drego surrounded by a bunch of lean black guys. Some wore brown-and-yellow armbands. These were the local dudes Drego had already said we couldn't trust.

Anja listening to her phone. She was nodding. Then she reached out and touched my arm. I looked at her and saw sadness in her smile. She said she was going into the van with Javier. We were both out of our element.

With the first sound of gunfire, the guys around Drego quickly parted, creating space between them. This was how you handled a drive-by shooting, I thought. No use letting one bullet hit two guys. Mei-Mei was with them, in the middle, wearing a short skirt that covered the top half of her fat thighs. She saw me looking at her, and for a moment we tried to make contact. Then I turned away.

Tristan was dragging barriers across the wide street using a jeep. It was all so crude. Translation: It was no longer a matter of board meetings or prostaglandin levels. It was about wood and metal to hide behind, steel vehicles and men with death and dying on their minds. I was scared out of my mind.

The battle. Down the street, less than a quarter mile away, they were coming. Young men, boys, wannabes with assault rifles, scrambling like dark insects past the parked cars, the streetlamps, the Dumpsters, toward us. They saw the barriers and stopped. Then they spread out across the street. Two of them were setting something up on the sidewalk that rimmed the park. A shot came from my left, and one of the boys near the park stood and tried to run. He was limping badly and soon fell. I hoped he'd been hit only in the leg. I hoped he wasn't going to die. My mouth went dry.

The raiders were retreating, scattering with the first wounded warrior. Then, suddenly, there was a roar that grew quickly. From where I crouched, kneeling on one knee, I saw a cloud of smoke headed toward us. It was twenty feet high, then thirty and still rising. It was a smoke screen that loomed like a friggin' nightmare in the distance, and it was growing. It became a moving cloud of black smoke that rose up a hundred or so feet, maybe more. At the base of the smoke, there were lights and grills.

They were driving cars toward us, shooting from the windows and from improvised holes in the tops of the vehicles. It was insane, until I heard the first bullets hit the steel barriers that Tristan had put up. The bullets rattled loudly against the barriers. The ones that missed the barriers, that whined and buzzed over our heads, were scarier.

The cars were zooming toward us. I thought they wanted to crash into the barriers, and I wondered if they were being driven automatically. The cars seemed too old, and I saw black hands firing from the windows. No one was firing back at them, and I didn't know what was going on.

Then all hell broke loose. From both sides there were *somethings* being shot across the road like the old pictures of snakes striking that I had seen in *National Geographic Classics*. They shot across, the ones from the park side going all the way over the wide road, the ones from the street side going three-quarters of the way. The *somethings* were black and weird-looking. And then they began to expand, and I saw that they were huge coils of barbed wire that expanded, and tangled, and bucked as if they were alive. When the first car hit the wire, it pushed the wire forward, then stopped, shuddered, and slowly was being pushed back. A dark figure jumped out of the car, then turned and ran as he realized that the wire, stretched by the car, was now recoiling toward him.

The wire hit the kid, lifted him off the street, and held him jerking spasmodically some fifteen feet above the tarred street.

There were more shots from the cars. They had all stopped and were shooting through the barbed wire. A few shots from our side had a deeper, more ominous sound. There were people running for cover. The smoke was clearing; they were trying to back the cars away. A few bodies lay on the ground just beyond the wire; a few more were caught in the wire. I was crying and I couldn't stop myself. Nothing made this right. The numbers could add up to what they needed to be and this would not be right. No, God, this would not be right!

There was nothing sure in this world. Drego could search for his soul all he wanted, but he couldn't erase the shadows of those bodies lying in this heat. Nothing could.

Silence. From time to time a cry for help. Was someone calling for his mother?

23

The gunfire had stopped. The overcast day had become suddenly brilliant. The barbed wire that had been shot across the road was dark and jagged against the lighter sky. There were still two bodies caught up in it. One of them was obviously young. He was thin, from a distance as black as the barbed wire, his body arched across the strands that cut into his flesh. There was a feeble effort by some of the people on his side of the wire to free him. From where we watched, we could hear his screams as the razors embedded in the wire cut more deeply into his flesh.

This was nothing like I had imagined. The neat dots on my computer screen were being translated into flesh and blood and the stink of gunfire.

Through the wire, I could see the other attackers begin to drift away. Some of them were crouching low as they hurried from the scene; others stood as they walked, in a futile display of bravado. They knew they were defeated. They hoped that they wouldn't be shot.

I saw Drego and went to him to ask if they would regroup and come back.

"No," he said. There was a catch in his voice. He was a hard shell of a man barely holding back the tears. "They're defeated. They'll slink away and look for something to get high on. That's what they're used to doing."

Minutes before—was it an hour?—Drego had been ready to do battle, and now he was saddened by what he had seen, pained. No matter what, they were his people. And he was right: slinking away was what they were used to, what we were all doing more and more.

A team of medics had arrived. No one on our side of the wire had been injured, and so they made their way to the deadly barrier and around it to the other side. Two of Tristan's crew went with them. They carefully lifted one of the kids off the wire and eased him down to the ground. I saw that one of the medics was a girl, thick-legged, plain. She was putting something on the black boy's legs. I guessed it was a topical anesthetic.

They checked the other body on the wire but quickly walked away. I looked at Drego and saw that Mei-Mei had her arm around his waist and was collapsed against his chest.

Michael came up to me, took my arm, and gently kissed

my shoulder. "You were on the money about how they would attack," he said. "Javier and Anja are trying to get the word out about what happened here, but we're being jammed."

"You think it's over?" I asked.

"The sooner they hear about how these guys were turned back, the sooner the rest of them will find something better to do than continue this attack," Michael said.

"That makes sense," I said. "But only from our point of view. We're still dealing with Sayeed and the guys he's brought with him from North Africa. They're not kids like the ones we just faced."

"But they'll see the wounded and think," Michael said. He was nodding as he spoke. "I'd see the wounded, and I know I would be asking myself if it was worth it."

"You can't *will* this to be over, Michael," I said. "There's got to be a *logic* to it. Sayeed has to come away with something, as Drego said. If he sacrifices a few more lives, he won't mind. You should know that."

"If we could get people flashing the word . . ." Michael looked around as if he was looking for an answer to pop up from behind a barrier, or from a sewer.

"It would help," I said.

"Are you sure that Sayeed's not through?" Michael asked.

"Yeah," I said. "I think he's not through. He uses the same equations as I do."

"I'll go tell Tristan and Javier."

It was weird watching Michael go off toward the command vehicle. I knew he had already had his fill of the fighting. It wasn't like being onstage, urging your band on and feeding off the frenzy of ten thousand screaming fans. It was looking out over a small field and seeing a dead body still in the wire and knowing you had something to do with its being there. It was reaching a point at which you couldn't just walk away anymore.

I wondered how many of the kids Sayeed had sent had actually been wounded. Tristan's guys had shot into the cars, and the return fire had ended quickly. The crashing into the wire barriers had been a foolish act of desperation, and had failed.

I felt so damned sad, so sorry for myself as I realized what I was doing. If I had seen the shit that was happening in Florida, if I had seen it on television or the Internet, I would have been disgusted. This was porn with the bodies still lying on the ground after the scene was over. And the truth was, I couldn't just turn it off, because I was part of it. I felt so sorry for myself, and at the same time I was mad, because I knew I should feel sorry for the kids Sayeed sent to fight his battle for him. The bastard!

Think, girl. I think, therefore I am!

I was thinking. We were being jammed, so there was no Internet coming in or phone messages going out. It was standard for C-8—control the flow of information and you control the battlefield. *But it had been done before!*

I stumbled as I ran over to where Drego and Mei-Mei

were standing. Next to him, in the street, she seemed tiny.

"Drego, Javier is trying to get the news out that the attack was beaten off," I said. "He thinks if we get it to the neighborhood, it'll keep other kids from joining Sayeed. The trouble is, somebody is jamming our signals. We can't spread the word. Are there any high-tech people in this area who can do countermeasures?"

"Countermeasures?"

"Override their jamming," I said.

"Let's find out."

We went to one of Tristan's guys and asked to borrow his vehicle. The guy waved, and two more of his kind, blond and buff, came over. They talked to each other, all the time looking at me, Drego, and Mei-Mei as if we were freaks. Finally they said yes.

"I'll stay here," Mei-Mei said.

I looked at her and saw her eyes as wide as I had ever seen them. She was scared shitless! Okay, not a problem. It was one thing to deal with this life as an academic exercise, or as a chess problem. That wasn't street life.

I got into the jeep with Drego, and we started driving into the downtown area.

"What happens if we get stopped?" I said. "A bunch of kids who just saw some of their friends get killed?"

"Then it's our turn to get killed," Drego said. He was looking down the street through the dusty windshield. He turned on the wiper control, and it spewed water onto the window and made it even harder to see through.

Drego drove quickly along the empty blocks. Everyone had heard the shooting, and nobody needed to be killed in a fight they didn't belong in. Count had been right: Sayeed hadn't picked up any local help.

There was a big twenty-four-hour clock on the dashboard. I watched the second hand sweep around a couple of times and was surprised when Drego slammed on the brakes in front of a corner building with a partially open steel folding gate.

"Play it hard," Drego said as he got out. "These people ain't got time for punks who ain't sure of themselves."

He pushed the gate all the way open and stepped inside the store. I felt a chill as I waited for the bullets to hit my body.

"Yo!" Drego shouted.

"What you want?!" I turned and saw a heavy black woman sitting on a stool in the corner. On the wall next to her was a picture of Papa Legba, the gatekeeper.

"I need to make a phone call and all the lines are jammed!" Drego said.

"Then you can't make no phone call." The woman's voice was flat, dry.

"I got fifty dollars." Drego.

"The phone is jammed." The woman was looking me up and down. "You can't make no phone call."

"Yeah, okay." Drego turned, brushed by me, and went toward the door. I followed.

"Let me see your fifty dollars."

We were back in the store, and the woman was counting

the money. She asked Drego if he had one hundred dollars. Drego spit, then ground the tip of his shoe into it.

The woman looked pissed but went to the shelf and pulled out what looked like the kind of remote control you find in cheap hotels. She handed it to Drego.

"Who we calling?" Drego asked.

I hadn't thought of that. "Can we reach the Brits?"

"You got a number?"

I took my phone out and found the number of the piss ant who wouldn't share his computer data. Drego dialed it as I recorded a text message into my own phone. I could hear the tones from the thing that Drego held going through relay switches. It took three minutes, which was good because I was able to record nearly a page of text.

"Carleton here."

"Carleton, this is Michael's group from the States," Drego said. "We've got a text message for you. Ready to receive it?"

"Of course."

I put my phone against the one that Drego held and pressed send. The message only took a second or two to transmit. Then I got on.

"We're cut off from regular communications," I said. "Michael needs somebody to get out the news that we've beaten back an attack. We don't know how many were killed or wounded, but the first attack by Sayeed and his people was beaten back."

"Killed or wounded?" Carleton. "Did you say 'killed or wounded'?"

"Yes."

"Cripes."

"We're expecting another attack," I said. "If I can, I'll let you know what happens. I think they're probably trying to regroup."

"Are you the girl?" Carleton.

The girl? "Yes, I'm the woman," I said.

"Do you think Michael should speak directly to Victor?"

Drego snatched the phone from my hand and let loose a string of curse words that included everyone in Carleton's family and the monkeys they came from. Then he told Carleton to have a blessed day and hung up.

"What was that phone device?" We were headed back to the area of the fight. "How come they can get through and we can't? What kind of tech shit is that?"

"It's called a land line," Drego said. "When they cut them down back in the day, people realized that the police could listen in on cell phones that went through the air, so they strung the telephone lines back up again. They go to a point outside the area, and then get picked up by cell from there."

"I didn't think they were that sophisticated," I said. "I mean technically."

"You kidding?"

I wasn't in the mood to spar with Drego. He knew a lot of stuff, but his ghetto act was wearing thin. Maybe it got him over with Mei-Mei, but I wasn't buying it.

Back at the command post. There were blogs coming through, hacked-in pop-ups on C-8's propaganda line. They were already talking about how the first attack had been turned away and added a bit about the "miracle" find in the United States.

HUSH-HUSH–MUSH-MUSH. MORE GLAD NEWS BEING FLUSHED DOWN THE TOILET IN THE YOU ESS OF HEY! BREAKTHROUGH SCIENCE–SOMETHING ABOUT CELL REGULATION–BEING HIJACKED AND STUFFED INTO THE PROFITS COLUMNS OF THE DEEP SIXERS. THE MYSTERIOUS DEATH OF A LOW-RANKING LAB WORKER, CONNECTED WITH CTI, POINTS TO A BEDTIME STORY– OTHERWISE KNOWN AS A COVER-UP. POLICE IN ST. PAUL, MINNESOTA, HAVE THEIR LIPS SEALED. THANK GOD THEY STILL HAVE THEIR POCKETS OPEN.

Michael was at my side and took my hand in his. His skin was softer than mine. "I'm thinking that if we retreat now, we can claim a victory," he said. "If Sayeed doesn't have an enemy, he can't have a victory."

"Enemies are just excuses," I said. "You want to do some evil shit, you look for somebody to make an enemy and then you do your shit. Sayeed came over here as a kickass African legend. He has to get back to neutral or he's going to lose everything he's spent his life building up."

"You're sure?"

"So are you," I said, "but some things we don't like to be sure about, right?"

"One day, if we're lucky, we'll look back on this and think it was all worth it," Michael said.

"Not if we're lucky," I said. "People are dying."

He dipped his head ever so slightly to one side. Then he walked away toward Javier's van.

24

Tristan. He had a slight stubble from not shaving for a few days. It was darker than the hair on his head, and it made him look rough. There was a translucent quality to his eyes. A gray-blue sky in autumn, but shallow.

"I know you think Sayeed's going to attack again," he announced. "But how will he attack?"

"He's unsure of himself," I said. "Usually he hangs back until there's a clear victory in sight. This time, he'll hang back even more. He might even try to make something of a defeat. I don't know for sure."

"That's not good enough," Tristan said. "Will he be in the attack or not?"

"No," I guessed, knowing how wrong I could be. "He only comes to the fight when he sees it's over. He'll hang around to see how it goes, and if it doesn't go right for his grand appearance, he'll look for an out. What I suspect, what I think, is that if things went against him in Morocco, he simply retreated into the mountains. He's not going to risk his neck here either."

"You'd make a great combat chick," Tristan said. "Somebody to plan battles with."

"Tristan, remember back in England, when we were the good guys? We were sitting in Dulwich College being all righteous and whatever?"

"Yeah?"

"And here we are fighting and killing street kids from Miami, the same kinds of people we're supposed to be saving," I said. "You see anything wrong with that?"

"My father used to say that the only way to talk to a snake is to first learn how to hiss," he said. "Sometimes people can't—or maybe won't—listen to you until they know you can speak their language as well as your own."

"And you're cool with that?"

"I can live with it," Tristan said. "I can live with it."

I think I'm losing the battle to save myself is what I wanted to say.

Tristan seemed less mindless as he walked off. I thought I knew him better now. He knew what he did. He was a fighter—he found his enemies and waged war, and he waited for the chance to do that. He needed me to say something, to allow him not to think about anything else, just to do what he did best. Fight. I knew him better, but I didn't know if I liked him as much.

We were waiting. Javier texted everybody that the

jamming had stopped. He wanted to know what that meant. Mei-Mei texted him back that C-8 was probably trying to limit their involvement. She had a grasp of things that I had to admire.

"A group of Sturmers has been spotted," Javier texted. "They are just to the left up ahead. Less than a mile away. They don't appear to be doing anything at this point."

Vultures, I thought.

We were waiting. I felt myself tensing up, felt the stiffness in my shoulders as I thought about what was to come. I imagined more old cars filled with high school dropouts moving toward the barriers, moving toward Tristan's people with their high-tech gear and square shoulders.

As few as we were, maybe fifty or so against three hundred that Sayeed might be able to muster, we were in the best position. On impulse I texted Mei-Mei.

D: What is the best endgame?

She texted me back.

M-M: Us being #alive#

Was that it? Was the best endgame only that we lived? What had I read about Martin Luther King, Jr.? That longevity had its place? I made a mental note to always hate Mei-Mei. Added that to the list of things I didn't like about her.

What I knew was that I hated Mei-Mei because she was right. I wanted to live. I wanted to know what was going to happen in the next few seconds, the next few minutes, the next hours. That was what made me human. Not the intelligence or the opposable thumbs. It was about finding out what happened next.

The fighting started again like a sudden spring rain, with big hard drops banging against the shutters. There were bullets hitting the barriers in front of us. I felt my legs and arms moving, scrambling like crazy to get closer to the protective metal shields. I was holding my breath, palms flat against the steel that I hoped would not let me die.

There was return fire from our side. The answers to the staccato fire, the high-pitched whines of bullets coming toward us, were the low and rumbling sounds of Tristan's men and their guns. The beasts had awakened.

I didn't want to, but somehow I forced myself to look around the steel barrier I had found. It was slightly shorter than me, about five feet high, with vertical slits to fire through. I looked, but I couldn't see anything. Who was shooting at us?

I could hear the sound of the shooting, could see the puffs of smoke and an occasional flash of light, but I couldn't see anyone holding a rifle or actually shooting in our direction. How could killing be so impersonal? An Asian dude with powerful arms and legs was giving orders over a phone. I wondered how he was giving orders to other people if he couldn't see shit.

"Armor!" The voice that called it out cracked as it rose.

I looked down the wide corridor again and saw four vehicles headed in our direction. They were tracked vehicles, lumbering and rumbling as they headed toward us.

The immediate response from our side, Tristan's army, was a wicked hissing noise followed by a boom that seemed to fill me up before knocking me down.

"Oh, my God!" Anja's voice. I looked up and saw she had her hands by the sides of her face as she looked down the street.

I looked. One of the vehicles had been hit. There were flames shooting high into the air. At the base of the flames there was still the outline of the vehicle, and a dark spot where it had been hit.

Another hissing noise, and I felt myself reaching for something to grab hold of. Too late. I had struggled to my feet, but now I was on the ground again. The blast from the gun had knocked me over. The sound seemed to be inside my body. I was shaking, and crying, and confused. I wanted to be away from where I struggled on the hard ground.

Another blast. I put my forehead down and felt it hit the black asphalt of the street. I wanted to puke as I pushed myself up to sit.

I saw a figure running across the road. It looked like a man, or a boy, maybe even a dog. Behind it there were the flaming hulks of two of the vehicles. Suddenly the silhouetted figure burst into flames. The figure still ran—I could make out the motion of sprinting legs, flailing arms. It was burning, but it still ran. Then it stopped.

More people, I pictured children, appeared from the brilliance of the flames. They ran a few steps and then, from where I sat flat on my ass and hurting, I could see them falling. Their arms always seeming to reach up to the sky before they hit the ground.

They had attacked, without a doubt on the strength of Sayeed's words, his promises that they would be all right. Now they were being slaughtered on the streets. I thought of how far away some of them were from home.

"Dahlia! Are you okay?" Anja's voice.

I turned and saw her running toward me. Then I saw one of her legs jerk up as she twisted, even as I was filled with a searing pain. Something tearing into my shoulder.

I was lying on the ground, Anja no more than inches away from me. She was moaning. Were we going to die here? God, how can you do this shit?

Hands picking me up. I was being carried. My shoulder hurt so bad. I was peeing all over myself.

I saw the van, and soon I was in the dark. I was lying on something, maybe a bench. Then there was light again and something was being laid beside me. I turned and saw it was Anja.

My shoulder was burning and I wanted to hit it, to put out the flames. I tried to look around, but there was nothing to see. I was trying to think of a prayer.

Hail Mary, full of grace, the Lord is with thee. Blessed art thou . . . "Oooh."

A moment went past. Two moments, maybe a thousand. I looked for Anja and saw her a few feet from me. She had gritted her teeth. They were small and white, and her lips were flat against her face.

There were guys shouting around me. The sounds of

the fighting went on, but in the darkness of the van, they seemed ever more far away.

Someone next to me. A Latino snipped away at my shirtsleeve.

"Not bad," he said. "A scratch. Nothing vital."

He was spraying me with something unbelievably cold, and the pain went away. I heard him saying something about how it was going to swell but that I'd be all right. It'd be more painful tomorrow, he reassured my hurt ass.

"Anja?"

I twisted up and saw that they had taken Anja's pants off. Her legs were white, and I saw she had an angry red crescent on her thigh. A kid with a roundish face sprayed her leg. Put his nose almost on the wound, sniffing. Then he took a paper square from a shelf, undid it, and put it on her wound.

"This will stop the bleeding," he said.

I looked at Anja's face, and she looked miserable. She saw me and forced a smile.

"I love you, Anja!" I called to her.

"We'll be okay," she said. It was what I needed to hear.

I was lying in what I recognized as the back of a medical van. On the wall, there was an illuminated strip. There were numerals on it. 4P2, 10 Mod 7, 3!, the square root of 81. A clock. I felt better. I didn't think I was going to die.

I saw Anja getting up, pulling herself together, pulling on her pants, and I swung my legs over the side of the platform I was lying on and got to my feet. Anja winced as she slipped back into her pants. The technician taped over the spot where he had cut them.

I steeled myself, ready to go outside again.

Outside. The sun was brilliant. The shadows on the ground were autumn-dark. There were few sounds except for the horrendous *whoosh*ing noise of our side's heavy weapons. The guys around me seemed relaxed. They looked at me and quickly looked away. I realized I was standing there in my bra. I banged on the door, and a guy opened it. He had my shirt in his hand, and I took it and put it on. As I twisted my shoulder, it hurt like hell.

Down the road where the attack started, the tracked vehicles were still burning. I wondered if there were still bodies in them. In the far distance, heat vapors rose toward the sky. The stench of the fighting—the fires, the gases from the guns—hung in the air.

To our left, across from the park, doors were opening. Slowly, people were coming out of their houses to see whatever they could. They were black and brown. They looked at us from across the grass and concrete field that separated us, and we kept a careful eye on them.

"Dahlia! Are you okay? How's the arm?" Michael. His hair was matted to his head, making a dark hieroglyphic over his forehead.

"Fine," I said.

"Tristan has Sayeed," Michael said. "I think he's going to kill him."

"He's captured him?"

Michael nodded.

"That's not right—the right thing to do," I said.

"Everybody thinks it is," Michael said, stepping closer to me. "He's caused the death of at least eight, maybe more, kids out here today."

"It's not the right thing to do!" I said emphatically. "We don't need to cross that line. What is it, revenge? We're writing history with us as the good guys, so everything we do is cool?"

He looked at me, his eyes widening; then he got on his phone. I could hear him calling Tristan. He turned away from me as he spoke into the phone. Then he turned back. "He hasn't killed him yet," he said. "If he doesn't kill him, then what?"

Think, Dahlia. What's the endgame? I didn't want to spend the rest of my life explaining to myself why I could be part of the street fighting and part of the bloodshed and still think I was a decent human being.

"Let the Sturmers take him," I said. "If the police want him, they can negotiate with those animals. They're all on the same side, really."

Michael let his arms drop to his side.

"Give Sayeed to the Sturmers," I said, this time more slowly.

Michael was on the phone as I walked away.

25

MIAMI HERALD

TURF WAR ERUPTS ON FRINGE OF "LITTLE HAITI." OVER A DOZEN KILLED, INCLUDING AFRICAN DRUG LORD AND INTERNATIONALLY KNOWN TERRORIST SAYEED IBN ZAYAD, WHO FELL AFTER A DESPER- ATE FIGHT WITH THE STURMERS. FBI DENOUNCES EFFORTS TO TIE AMERICAN DRUGGIES WITH FOR- EIGNERS.

LONDON EVENING NEWS

Americans answer violence the way they usually do, greater violence that carries the day! Should we be thankful?

PHOEBE'S SCREAM MACHINE

When Natural Farming placed its company logo between two shining moons, they wanted to tell the world that they were the truth and the light. But a bunch of teenagers, including one heavy rocker and one South Chicago gangbanger (not known if Crips or Bloods), showed that it was just the Big Company with its pants down!

El Bronx. Four-thirty in the morning. A hazy moon hung over the dark silhouettes of the warehouses. Below, the all-night *restaurante y bodega* was still open, the yellow-orange light from its window lying like a stain on the sidewalk. The smell of pulled pork and plantains was only a memory, but it still made me hungry. An old man came out of the store carrying a plastic bag, and I imagined it held what was left of the day's roti.

There was a light rain; it was only slightly cold. It started and stopped every few minutes. My mother used to call this kind of rain "angel piss."

Across from me I saw a woman looking out from the window. Half hidden by the curtain—her hair, straight, long, and silver, gave her away. How many things had she seen on this street? I retreated from the window, took a pillow from my bed, and put it on the windowsill. Then I put my arms on it and leaned out to see the street more clearly. I didn't look at the woman.

Michael had asked me to stay with him and the others in Morristown, but I needed to get away. None of my numbers added up to anything I could call truth. They just led me to other equations, other problems, other what-ifs. And even as I saw why my numbers didn't arrive at any great and clear truth, I could also see how C-8 could add their numbers and think they had a holy friggin' grail. They were looking for profits, and more was always there for them, always available. The answers they looked for were just a damned lot easier than mine.

I wondered if I would ever come up with one true answer that would tie everything together. Could be, but right now I didn't have it. Later, I would go with my gut, but for now I still wanted to go with my brain. I would analyze everything carefully and try not to lie to myself, even though I knew that there were lies waiting to comfort me.

"Don't give in to them, girl," I told myself. That made me smile. Here I was in my tiny apartment in the South Bronx talking to myself.

I thought about our little band.

Tristan was simple. For him everything was either right or wrong. There was nothing in between. I envied him. I was nothing if not my in-betweens. He was good-looking, with a detachment about him that reminded you of a Scottish moor or an angry, moody sea. That was his charm, really. The aloofness. You wanted to cross to get where he was, to be near him, but he wouldn't let that happen. Even his arrogance worked for him.

Drego didn't fool anyone. He was all street and all mean-smart. He sensed moves, like a boxer or a dancer. I thought he fought against his feelings. I wondered, when he was alone, maybe sitting on the john or lying awake at three in the morning, if he thought about the woman he had hit in Miami, or the people he had dealt with down there. I knew he looked at the kids who had been killed as just that—kids who had been killed. I knew they ate at his soul.

Javier. Smart, hurting. He held a memory of Ellen, of the life that could have been. How hard must that shit have been? To never have had that slice of life that you thought would have been fulfilling, and be doomed to forever long for it. Ellen was as much a part of Javier as the Bronx was part of me. I relied on the Bronx, pretended that I didn't love it, but I kept coming back. I kept coming back.

Anja was so cool. She found people out. We were all naked to her. When she looked at me, I thought she saw deeper than anyone I had ever met. She knew who I was, where I lived, where all my flaws were hidden, and how my juices flowed. Yes, I sweated, and I peed, and I cried, and she knew all of it, all about me. Her knowing made me glad. It was good to have someone who knew you without having to climb over the mountain of what you had to say, or the disguises you put on or the dances you did. She saw people for what they were, naked and alone, and needing each other. I thought she was a good person. Maybe a saint. Maybe just her knowing so much about me, where the truth lay in me, let me love her.

Mei-Mei. She had invented herself, had given herself all kinds of crazy skills, and knew everything. It was so stupid for me to say that I would like to fight her, but I kept thinking about it. Just one punch to that cute little face would have done me so much good.

She was also bitchy, which was the only part of her I liked.

Michael. Brought us into his magical world and stepped back so that we could each bring our own melodies and rhythms to the jam. We each saw the illusions on the wall and made our own interpretations, but in the end we pulled it together, learned to respect each other, and stopped the great beasts of almighty profit from devouring more of us. At least we had done it for the moment, at least for this time, and for the few places in which the shadows had been made brighter.

In a perfect world, a boy-meets-girl kind of world where there was blushing and sneaky looks across the room and body parts coming together in hot moments, I could have sweated Michael big-time. There was something about him that called my name even if I was half scared to answer him. If I had gone off with him to climb the mountain, I don't know what I would have told Mrs. Rosario when I got back.

Michael, Drego, Tristan, Javier, Anja, Mei-Mei, and me, we were a good team. Together, we'd learned what we could do. C-8 had backed off from acquiring another company. For now. We had won. But I thought we might have learned not to question what we had won.

Some of the medical people from CTI were finally speaking out. And there was a three-page blog out of Johns Hopkins about how more research was needed to verify the prostaglandin findings.

I wondered if I was still young enough, still hopeful and innocent enough, to think about going to medical school.

And then there was Lydia, who was smart. The way she looked at me and Anja, reaching out to us intellectually, wanting to have faith in her intelligence, it meant a lot to me. Little girls need to grow up to be smart, involved women. Little boys, too. One day, if Lydia found out all that we did, it would be worth it to me.

But we did some bad shit too. How bad? Bad enough for me to run back to the Bronx and sit in my little den and boo the fucking hoo all over the place and wonder who I was again.

We killed. Stop. Don't fancy the shit up. We killed, left bodies lying in the streets in the name of peace. The fact that I could still find my soul in the middle of all my doubts didn't help for more than a few minutes at a time.

In the end, I hoped we were better, that we were more righteous than the drug dealers and the money lords and all the fools running around allowing themselves the luxury of ignorance. How much is two plus two? Can you really not know?

Maybe the Gaters were the real enemy. People who closed their eyes to what was happening, who allowed themselves to unknow what they damn well knew, who allowed their petty comforts to come at a price that thousands—millions of people—had to pay. The real enemy was their indifference.

Maybe. Who knows?

Hey, and what would I do? Go back to my math, to

my numbers, to my equations, trying to make sense of it all. If Michael called me today, or tomorrow, I would probably go back to him. I'd use my skills and hope I was on the right side. It'd be a chance to be, to live, to stake out my humanity. Maybe Michael would look at me and see something—someone—Dahlia—as being very special. Maybe he'd fall in love with me so hard, his nose would bleed and he'd come begging at my feet. I could use some of that.

The sky was becoming lighter. A broad beam of light promised sunshine. I could see the clouds now, and they were breaking up. Perhaps it would be a clear day.

In the window opposite me, the woman disappeared, and then she reappeared with a pillow. She put it on the windowsill and put her arms on it.

I waved to her. My arm was still hurting.

She waved back.

WALTER DEAN MYERS

1937–2014

WALTER DEAN MYERS'S fiction and nonfiction books have reached millions of young people. A prolific author of more than one hundred titles, he received every major award in the field of children's literature. He wrote two Newbery Honor Books, eleven Coretta Scott King Author Award and Honor Books, three National Book Award finalists, and the winner of the first Michael L. Printz Award for Excellence in Young Adult Literature. He also received the Margaret A. Edwards Award for lifetime achievement in writing for young adults and was the first recipient of the Coretta Scott King–Virginia Hamilton Award for Lifetime Achievement. He was a 2010 United States nominee for the Hans Christian Andersen Award and was nominated for the Astrid Lindgren Award numerous times. From 2012 to 2013, he served as the National Ambassador for Young People's Literature with the platform "Reading is not optional."

When asked about his readers, Walter would often say, "Young people are some of the best people I know." In Walter's short-story collections *145th Street* and *What They*

Found, he celebrates a community of people in a Harlem neighborhood. His novels *Hoops* and *The Outside Shot* appeal especially to basketball fans. Walter set *On a Clear Day* in the future and gave it a global context because "it's never too soon for young people to bring their awareness and energy to the world's problems. . . . [Ultimately] the teens in *On a Clear Day* want to make a difference." In his most-beloved books, Walter explored the theme of taking responsibility for your life while reminding readers that everyone *always* gets a second chance.

DON'T MISS...

A Conversation with
Walter Dean Myers, Author,
and Phoebe Yeh, Publisher

. . .

Excerpt from *145th Street*

. . .

Excerpt from *Hoops*

A CONVERSATION WITH WALTER DEAN MYERS, AUTHOR, AND PHOEBE YEH, PUBLISHER

Phoebe Yeh: Walter, why did you give your novel a global setting?

Walter Dean Myers: I really believe the world is shrinking every day! What happens in any part of the world affects us all, and multinational corporations are using this to their advantage in their drive for profits. In *On a Clear Day*, some of the smartest kids in the world realize their future is at stake, stand up, and do something about it.

PY: Where did you get the idea for the book?

WDM: I saw a line of teenagers, nearly a half block long, waiting outside of a store to buy the latest athletic shoes. I had an image of exhausted workers in Asian sweatshops making shoes to ship halfway around the world to American markets. Making their workers happy clearly wasn't on the agenda of the "good guys" who owned the factories.

PY: Why did you decide to write about a heroine?

WDM: I saw part of the Occupy Movement in London. I thought the movement needed more than the slogans they were spouting or the raised fists. Dahlia was my answer. She started out as a minor character who has crazy mad math skills, but as I looked at her picture on the wall of characters behind my computer, Dahlia began to grow on me. I realized that I didn't just want to say that corporations were heartless. I wanted to create a sympathetic character who had empathy for others and could channel her behavior and others' in a mathematical way.

PY: You have also given Dahlia companions, among them an ex-rocker, an ex-con, and a chess prodigy. How did you decide on a mix of personalities?

WDM: In a Q&A session in a juvenile prison, one young inmate who had art skills asked me how he could break into book illustration. Another inmate answered the question by asking the budding artist if he had a portfolio, and the two began to exchange ideas. I realized how great it would have been if the two young men could have combined their skills and knowledge before they got into trouble. So for this book, I created characters with diverse skills who appreciate and trust each other's abilities.

PY: And we have Sayeed, a teen terrorist.

WDM: What happens when a person is clever, charismatic, and dedicated to making a difference in his life and the lives of his people, but doesn't have the sophistication or resources to do so peacefully? Often he becomes a terrorist, using the weapons at hand, with a studied disregard for personal sacrifices. Ultimately, the compromises Sayeed makes in resorting to violence and the gun culture also bring about his destruction.

PY: Full disclosure: I didn't know anything about computer modeling until I read this book.

WDM: Computer modeling is a growing field. It's used to predict epidemics, economic trends, the effects of deforestation, and medical projections. We're becoming more adept at collecting data and using it intelligently.

Today's teenagers don't have to wait fifteen years to see the effects of climate change; they can model the changing weather patterns and predict exactly what the world will look like when they become its principal caretakers.

PY: Is this novel a call to action for teens?

WDM: George Orwell's excellent novel *1984* was published in 1949, only thirty-five years before the title date. But Orwell saw that some of the remarkable events of the novel were already taking shape. It's clear to me that many giant corporations already control large segments of our lives and threaten to become even more intrusive and manipulative if we allow them. Our teens will either be co-conspirators by ignoring the global intentions of these companies (think teenagers lining up to buy athletic shoes made by exploited workers in another country) or will involve themselves in being part of the much-needed solutions to counter corporate power. It's never too soon for young people to bring their awareness and energy to the world's problems.

PY: From 2012 to 2013, you served as National Ambassador for Young People's Literature. Your platform was "Reading is not optional." What did you learn from traveling around the country?

WDM: The skills needed to survive are changing. Today's young people need excellent reading skills to move ahead with their lives. Just getting by *doesn't* get you by anymore. When I was traveling, I saw great schools and great students. But too many young people seem to be alienated from both school and society. The teens in *On a Clear Day* want to make a difference.

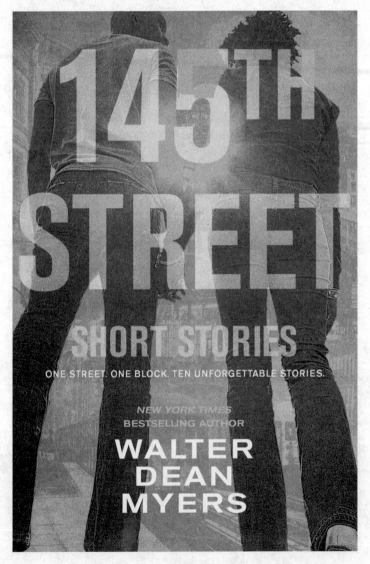

145TH STREET

SHORT STORIES

ONE STREET. ONE BLOCK. TEN UNFORGETTABLE STORIES.

NEW YORK TIMES
BESTSELLING AUTHOR

WALTER
DEAN
MYERS

Kitty and Mack: A Love Story

Eddie McCormick was all-world and everybody knew it. While most of the guys on the block played basketball, Mack, which was what everybody called him, played baseball. He played left field for the Ralph Bunche Academy and when they played there would be more scouts in the stands than fans. He was big, a hundred and eighty pounds and six feet one. During the winter he ran track and the track coach thought he could make the Olympics if he stuck with sprinting. The coach kept him on the team even when he wasn't running, just in case he might show up at a meet. But baseball was Mack's joint and that was where he figured to be headed. He was eighteen and one newspaper article about him said that he could be in the major leagues by the time he was nineteen. That's how good he was. Naturally the baseball coach loved him. That was the thing about Mack, the people who liked him usually liked him because he was a star. Mack had an attitude problem. He thought he could just show up and everybody was supposed to fall down and go crazy or something.

He was pretty smart, too, but he made this big show of not caring about grades. He slid into his senior year with a C-minus average.

"If they gave him what he really deserved," Dottie Lynch said, "he would be getting all P's. That's *P* as in *pitiful.*"

Well, Dottie had a big mouth but that's what people thought about Mack. Some of the kids thought that Dottie was sweating Mack and was just mad because he didn't give her a play. On the other hand everybody thought he was stuck on himself. But during the first week of his senior year everything changed. That's when he met Kitty.

Kitty was the granddaughter of Duke Wilson, who owned the barbershop on 145th across from Grace Tabernacle Church. Now, anybody who knew Mr. Wilson would expect his granddaughter to be smart, but Kitty was outrageous. Just the way that Mack dealt with baseball and had all the scouts looking at him, Kitty could deal with the books. What's more, everybody liked Kitty because she had one of those bubbling kind of personalities that soon as you met her you knew she was your flavor. Plus, the girl was fine. Not just kind of fine, not just take another look fine, but, like, take the batteries out of the smoke alarms when she came by fine. Yeah, that's right. So she's smart, she's fine, she's only sixteen and a senior.

Okay, the first week of school Mrs. Henry, our English teacher, said we had to write poems in the style of some famous poet. And you had to write the poem to a particular person.

"It can be someone you admire," Mrs. Henry said. "Someone you're in love with, or even someone to whom you just want to send a message."

The boys all treated the assignment like it was a big goof and most of the girls weren't too excited about it, either. On the day the poems were read in class it was mostly funny stuff or poems about how they loved their mothers. Three people wrote poems about Martin Luther King, Jr. Half the class just listened to the poems and hoped they wouldn't be called on to read theirs out loud. But when it was time for Kitty to read her poem, she said, "I'm going to read my poem to Mack."

Everybody paid attention.

Mack leaned back in his seat and got this look on his face like he was too cool to breathe. Okay, Kitty went and stood right in front of Mack and started reciting her poem real slow. She was just glancing at the paper it was written on but most of the time she was looking dead into Mack's eyes.

"How do I love thee, you sweet black thing
Why do I love thee, is this some fling
That my wildly beating heart has chanced
Upon or has my light and joyous soul danced
With yours in some other life or taken wing
And flown with yours, you sweet black thing."

The class was quiet and Mrs. Henry put her book down and sat behind her desk. Kitty went on with her poem.

"How do I love thee, my sweet black prince
For surely I have loved thee ever since
My eyes first met your fierce but tender gaze
And your gentle touch did expand my days
As poets' songs fulfill the singing verse
And sweet love fulfills the universe.

"I haven't finished it yet," Kitty said. "It's going to be a sonnet."

She hadn't finished the sonnet but she had finished Mack. From that minute on he was stupid in love. What she did was to flat-out change the brother. She had reached inside him and took out his attitude. Peewee put it best.

"What Mack was doing was dealing wrong but dealing so strong you couldn't do nothing about it," he said. "But how strong can you be when some girl can make you roll over and play dead any time she wants to? She can make that dude fetch like a cocker spaniel if she wanted."

That was true, because Mack would be in the cafeteria or walking down the hallway and all of a sudden this silly grin would come over his face and either Kitty would be someplace near or he would be thinking about her. Mack was so much in love that it made people feel good just to be around him. He was talking about going right to the major leagues and playing pro ball while Kitty went to school.

They went out steady for a while and after a few weeks Kitty naturally wanted to know how Mack felt about her. She hinted around for a while, then she came right out and asked him.

"You're okay," he said.

"Don't give me no okay," Kitty said. "I want to know if you love me."

"Something like that," Mack said.

That's what he said to Kitty, but to everybody else he was planning his whole life.

"It'll take her six or seven years to get her law degree," he said. "Then I'll play ball for another eight or nine years and then we'll open a little business."

Kitty lived with her parents above her grandfather's shop. That's where Mack was coming from the day before Christmas. Kitty had been up at Brown University in Rhode Island on a visit to see if she wanted to go to that school and Mack had met her at the train station. It was a cold night and a light snow was falling. Down on the corner some guys were selling Christmas trees and had started a fire in a garbage can to keep warm.

All of a sudden two guys come running down the street. They were hoofing heavy and looking back over their shoulders. When they ran across Powell Avenue they almost got hit by a gypsy cab. The cab swerved just in time and one brother was slipping on the snow and almost fell in the path of a delivery truck. He was so close to being hit that he steadied himself on the fender of the truck. The car that came across the intersection was an old Mustang painted black. The two guys were running on the uptown side of the street but the Mustang came over, facing the wrong way in traffic, and a dude leaned out the back window.

"Drive-by!" a kid screamed.

People were hitting the ground, or running, or ducking behind cars. Most of them didn't know where the shooting was coming from. A window broke, sending glass across the sidewalk. People screamed. Tires squealed. The two guys they were shooting at turned the corner and ran up the avenue. The car sped away toward the bridge that leads to the Bronx. In a minute it was out of sight.

"That's a shame!" an old West Indian woman was saying.

"Those gang people don't care two cents for your life!" the woman with her said.

"The day before Christmas, too," the first woman went on, shaking her head. "They don't have a thing to do but to—is that somebody laying on the ground over there?"

It was Mack. A man called the police and in minutes the street was full of police cars and emergency vehicles.

"He's moving," a long-headed boy with a scarf around his face said. "He's okay."

They took Mack downtown to Harlem Hospital. Pookie, who came along after the shooting and saw that it was Mack, went and told his folks.

It was Christmas day when the news got back to the block. Mack was going to live, but two bullets had torn into his right ankle and just about taken his foot off. Doctors had worked on his foot for seven hours, but finally they gave up. It had to be amputated.

When he came out of the hospital Mack was different. It wasn't like he just acted a little strange; he was a different person. At first when some of the guys went around to see him they said he didn't talk much, but then after a while he wouldn't even come out of his room. Then Peewee found out that he hadn't seen Kitty.

"She didn't even go to the hospital?" Eddie, who was in Mack's math class, asked.

"She went to the hospital," Peewee said. "But since he's been home he hasn't seen her. He told his mother not to let her in and he won't answer the phone."

"You can't turn your back on people like that," Eddie answered.

But the truth was that Mack could turn his back on people, because he really had turned his back on himself. Kitty called him every day at the same time so he would know it was her, but he wouldn't answer.

Mack's father worked in a restaurant just down from Sylvia's. It wasn't as high-class a restaurant as Sylvia's but it was nice. He went to work at one in the afternoon and Mack would keep his door closed, not even come out of his room, until after his father had left.

The next thing that Kitty did was to organize a little get-together with Peewee and some of the guys on the baseball team. Peewee told me about it and for the first time he didn't make a lot of jokes about it.

"He was sitting on his bed and he had his leg out from under the cover," Peewee said. "You know, we just sat there and tried not to look at his leg. Mack kept laughing at his leg and pointing to it. Man, it was terrible. Dottie was there and she held Kitty's hand."

"She was tore up," Dottie said. "You loving somebody like she loves that fool and you hate to see them looking so pitiful."

"Nobody else could get it up to say anything," Peewee continued. "People started drifting out one by one. I know those guys aren't going back there. That scene was too rough."

No one saw Mack for a long time after that. There were reports that he had lost a lot of weight, and that maybe he was losing his mind. The worst time was when Mack's father called the cops because he wouldn't come down from the roof. It was nearly three o'clock in the morning in late January. A cold rain slanted down onto the tar paper and onto the lone figure sitting on the ledge overlooking the empty street below. A policeman tried to talk him away from the edge but Mack didn't respond.

"Why, son, why?" his father pleaded with him. "You're young and still got your whole thing going on in front of you. I know it's not like it was but you're still young."

"Who?" Mack spoke without moving.

At first his father just looked at him, not knowing what his son was getting at. "What you mean who?" his father asked.

EXCERPT FROM *HOOPS*

NEW YORK TIMES
BESTSELLING AUTHOR

WALTER
DEAN
MYERS

BASED ON AN ORIGINAL SCREENPLAY BY JOHN BALLARD

I have a funny way of thinking—at least I think it's funny because I don't hear anybody else saying they think the way I do. What I do is to think things part of the way out, and then I put them aside and think them out some more later on. I had begun to think about what my father had said a long time ago about your days piling up on you, and as I sat in the window of the Grant, I began thinking about it again. It was beginning to make more sense to me.

School was going to be out in another five or six weeks, and then I was going to have to figure out something to do with myself. Before, I'd spend the summer playing ball and waiting around until school started again, so that would take care of itself. But now that school was just about over for me, the days seemed different, and I had to figure out what I was going to do with them. I knew I didn't want to work at the Grant all the time. I hated Jimmy Harrison, the manager, and the job was a chump job anyway—sweeping floors and changing beds and that kind of thing. The only thing that made it not so bad was me telling myself it was just until I finished school. I saw a lot of guys who had either finished school or had dropped out just hanging around the block, and I didn't want to do that either. I wondered if my days were piling up on me, like my father said they might. They were changing, at least, or maybe I was changing. Or was supposed to be and wasn't.

I sat in the window for a long time, and then I laid across the bed, just waiting for time to pass. I dozed off for a while, and when I woke, it was just about dark. I thought about going to a movie but decided to save my money so I could go the next day in case it rained. I got a basketball I kept at the Grant and wandered over to the playground. The lights were on, and I figured I'd shoot a few baskets. Playing ball, even shooting baskets by myself, always made me feel better. I figured to shoot until I got tired and then come back and get some sleep.

I had my head so wrapped up in myself I didn't see this guy laying on the court until I got right up on him.

"Hey, man." I nudged him with the toe of my sneaker. "Get off the court!"

When he didn't move, I thought he might be dead. I nudged him again.

"Your feet too big . . ." That's what he said, only he kind of sung it instead of talking.

"Hey, man, get up!"

"I really hate you 'cause your feet too big . . ."

The cat is laying there singing some kind of weird song. I pushed him with my sneaker again, and he didn't move. So I gave him a kick on the back of his leg and told him to move again. He rolled over and got up on his knees and hands like a boxer trying to beat the count. I thought he was getting right up, but he just stayed like that for a while. I reached down and grabbed him by the collar and started to drag him off the court, and then, all of a sudden, he's up. Not only is he up, but he's got this blade in my face!

I dropped the ball and backed off. This guy smells like somebody done peed in bad wine and washed his teeth in it, but he's got this knife, and he's bigger than me.

"Hey, why don't you get off the court, man?" I said.

"I really hates you 'cause your *feets* too big . . ." He starts in with this singing again, and I just watched him. I didn't want to get too close to him 'cause I still didn't know where he got the knife from and he was quick.

He stops just before he gets off the court and turns back to me and just looks at me, and then he puts his knife away. Right away I feel like busting his jaw. I take a step toward him, and he just grins at me.

"Get off the court, old man, before I hit you!"

"Why don't you put me off the court, youngblood?" he says, still grinning.

I look at him for a minute, and he don't look like much. But I'm six three and he's maybe six four, and he's heavier. I wasn't scared of the cat, but I figured it wasn't worth my while. I could hit him and he'd have a heart attack and die and I'd be up for manslaughter or something.

I picked up the ball and shot it. He turned and walked off, still singing that stupid song about feet. I shot a few times, and then the ball came down on something—a broken bottle of wine. I started to push it off the court with my foot, but then I picked it up and threw it off as far as I could. I got the ball again and shot and shot until I was too tired to shoot anymore. Then I took the ball over to the track and ran laps until I could see the sky start turning gray between the buildings.

The next morning Harrison had me cleaning rooms with him and listening to a lot of guff about how hard he had it when he was my age. He'd heard that I was the first to cop from the truck the day before and asked me where I was keeping my stash.

"Don't worry about it," I told him.

He gave me a look hard enough to curdle water and went on sweeping. After we finished cleaning the rooms, I split to Mary-Ann's house.

Mary-Ann is just about my woman. Just about, because I haven't really done anything to make it official.

I've known Mary-Ann and her brother Paul just about all my life. For a long time I treated her like a younger sister. Paul and I were close, too. If I had to call somebody my main man, he'd be it. We were just about the same age and had been going to school together, eating at each other's house and stuff like that for as long as I can remember. Lately Paul had been hanging around with some of the cats at school who thought they were better than the rest of us. This was a new thing with him, and I couldn't figure it, but I gave him the benefit of the doubt.

Mary-Ann was something else. She had been Paul's kid sister and I had liked her, and then one day she just wasn't a kid anymore. I don't know if she just changed or if both of us did. I remember being at Paul's house one day, waiting for him to finish his shower, and Mary-Ann and I were playing checkers. I used to always let her beat me, and then I'd sneak a checker off the table and we'd wrestle around for it. Only this time, when she tried to wrestle me to the floor to get the checker out of my hand, I was suddenly aware that she was a woman. I opened my hand real quick, and she asked me what was wrong, was I getting weak? I just looked at her and she looked at me and we both knew things had changed between us.

I found myself liking her more and more, but I tried to keep it cool. I wasn't really ready for no big love thing, but I liked the way I felt around her, and she knew it, even though I never said it in so many words.

When I got over to Paul's house, he wasn't home. Mary-Ann and her mother were there, mouthing off at each other like they always did.

About six months before, they had been arguing about the fact that Mary-Ann didn't get a new coat for Christmas. Her mother came back with how bad things were and how much this cost and how much that cost and the usual noise people be handing out when they come up short. Then she starts saying that since Mary-Ann had just turned sixteen, she could go out and get her a part-time job or something and help get her own stuff. I guess she figured that Mary-Ann would work in the supermarket or something like that. But there's an after-hours joint across from where Paul lives, and Mary-Ann gets a job there instead.

Mary-Ann's job was to keep track of the liquor and stuff so that the bartenders wouldn't rip off the money from the sales. She ordered stuff like peanuts, and potato chips, too. But her mother kept running down about how Mary-Ann was going to be a tramp because she worked in the after-hours joint, especially when the dude that ran it gave Mary-Ann her own room. Mary-Ann told her mama that the guy wanted her to stay there some of the time so in case he wanted to check things out, she could tell him what was what. Her mama didn't want to hear a thing, so she just kept running the same old lines. Mary-Ann was making about three times as much as she could in the supermarket and she dug the responsibility, so she wasn't about to give up the gig.

After she and her mother had finished putting each other down, we went down and sat on the stoop.

"She just stays on my case," Mary-Ann said. Her eyes were red, and I figured she was ready to cry.

"You know what she's going to say," I said, "so just get used to it."

"I don't dig her always accusing me of 'getting ready to do some dirt,'" Mary-Ann said. "If her stuff wasn't so raggedy, she wouldn't have the dirt on her mind."

"Why I got to hear this?" I asked. "I've heard it a hundred times, and it don't change none."

"Who else I got to say it to?"

"Ease up, mama," I said. "I didn't come to start nothing. I just came over to see what Paul was doing, that's all. Look, you want to catch a flick this afternoon?"

"I got to work," she said. "She always waits until I'm just about out the door before she starts running her mouth."

"All that means I got to go to the flick by myself?"

"You want to see me when I get off work?"

"I'll think about it."

"Jive turkey!" She got up and gave me a smile that made me glad that Paul hadn't been home. I watched her cross the street and head down the block towards the after-hours joint, knowing that she would turn around before she went in. She got all the way to the door and then turned and threw me a kiss. I threw one back underhanded, and she disappeared into the doorway.

I went back over to the Grant to get my sneakers. I had heard that they were looking for some ball-players for some kind of tournament or something. At the Grant there's Harrison sitting behind the desk, writing up a card for some dude and a white chick. The chick wasn't bad. I'm just going to walk on by the desk when I see a bottle of Johnnie Walker Black, half gone, sitting against the wall. So I wait until this cat and his white chick go on upstairs, and I sound on

Harrison. I know that better not be my stuff or I'm going to waste him right then and there.

"Hey, man, you drinking top shelf," I said, pointing to the Johnnie Walker.

"I don't like nothing cheap," he said.

"Well, that ain't cheap," I said. "Wherever you get it from it's going to cost you."

"That right?"

The way he said that I just knew it was my stuff he was drinking. I just *knew* it.

"Look, man, you going to be here long?" I asked. "Because I'm going to go upstairs and check something out, and then I'll be right back down if everything isn't everything."

"Your mama was by here a few minutes ago," he said.

"Say what?"

"I said that your mama was by here a few minutes ago. She said she was sorry to bother you again, but the landlord came and said that she either had to pay the rent or leave the place. I figured since it wasn't that much, I could lend her the money."

I just looked at him and he looked at me. Then he reached over and poured himself another drink. I didn't say anything else. I went on upstairs and looked under the bed and pulled out the box. There were two bottles of Scotch left. When I came down again, I asked him how much he had lent my mama.

"Don't worry about it," he said, "you'll pay it back."

"Hey, look, can I ask you a question?"

"Free country."

"Do you practice being stupid, or is it just natural?"